SHERLOCK HOLMES
AND THE
EXPLORERS' CLUB

The Early Casebook of Sherlock Holmes

Book Two

Linda Stratmann

SAPERE
BOOKS

SHERLOCK HOLMES
AND THE
EXPLORERS' CLUB

Published by Sapere Books.

24 Trafalgar Road, Ilkley, LS29 8HH
United Kingdom

saperebooks.com

ISBN: 978-1-80055-483-2

To Michelle and Tom and the man on the horse.

From
Memoirs of a Medical Man
by A. Stamford FRCS

1924

CHAPTER ONE

London, 1876

There is a bond which forms between men who have saved each other's lives. Sherlock Holmes and I were of that brotherhood, yet for some time after the adventure of the Rosetta Stone which I have already recounted, we saw little of each other. Holmes went into a period of languor during which he was only occasionally seen at Barts, and I was devoting almost all my time to my medical studies. The long vacation, a greater part of which I spent in Greece with my new friend, classics scholar George Luckhurst, opened my eyes to the art and culture of ancient civilisations. When I returned to Barts for the winter session in October, I saw Holmes back in his usual place in the laboratory and we greeted each other but without any great effusion of delight. We would never, I realised, become close friends. We were too different.

In the colder months, the students' reading room, which occupied a remote corner in the basement of Barts, was a cosy retreat, its principal comforts being a warm fire, easy chairs, copies of recent periodicals and an absolute ban on smoking and the consumption of refreshments. From time to time it hosted meetings of the Abernethian Society, named after Sir John Abernethy, the founder of the college, and inventor of the nutritious biscuit which bears his name. Members of the society presented papers for discussion on such wide-ranging subjects as unusual foreign objects they had discovered inside patients and the many varieties of delirium. I recall a particularly contentious debate on the usefulness or otherwise of the recently introduced practice of using antiseptics in the treatment of wounds. We students were also regularly regaled with exhibitions of diseased organs and misshapen limbs.

That winter, one paper in particular attracted my attention. A third-year student called Danville displayed a preserved foot which was provided with an unusual number of toes, seven in all, one of the additional digits being fully articulated. The other foot, we were told, had been quite normal in appearance. It belonged to a man who had been brought into the hospital a few weeks earlier after being crushed under the wheels of a cab. His injuries had been extremely severe, and he had died shortly afterwards. The dead man had nothing on his person which could identify him. His description was published in the newspapers, and many people had come to view the body, the torn and bloodstained clothes, crumpled hat, muddy boots, and few simple possessions, but no-one had claimed him, or so much as suggested a name. Unfortunately, his face had been so bruised and swollen by the accident it was feared that even a close relative would not have been able to recognise him, and as the days passed his appearance did not improve. The unclaimed body had therefore been given up for dissection in the medical college.

I wondered if Holmes might be able to use his remarkable skills to identify the deceased man, if, that is, he would find sufficient stimulation for his mind in such a trivial mystery. When I went to find him, however, I learned that he had recently experienced a failure in one of his chemistry experiments and had not been seen in the laboratory since. I sought out Danville and established that the corpse, once it had made its contribution to the study of medicine, had been buried, and the clothing burnt, but the dead man's boots and the contents of his pockets had been retained in case anyone might come to name him. I decided to call upon Holmes at his rooms in Montague Street.

I found Holmes reclining on his sofa in a dressing-gown, his eyes closed, while puffing away on one of his dreadful clay pipes. The grey pall of smoke surrounding him suggested that he had done little else for some time. The room was in its usual state of disarray, with open books and newspapers piled about the floor.

'Are you well, Holmes?' I enquired.

'I am,' he said languidly. 'However, my researches have reached an impasse and I need to give the problem further thought before I can proceed. I am having a very tedious time of it, and I fear I will be tedious company.'

'I have just learned of an interesting mystery, and I thought it might amuse you to solve it,' I said.

He turned his face towards me, his eyes heavy-lidded slits, then he tilted his head back drowsily and said, 'Go on.'

I explained about the unidentified body of the man with the extra toes.

At the end of my speech, I thought for one moment that Holmes had fallen asleep, but then he said, 'And his possessions are still available for examination?'

'Only his boots, and a few things found in his pockets.'

'One may learn a great deal about a man from his boots, or his hat, or his pipe,' observed Holmes. Despite the leisurely manner of his speech, I sensed that his interest had been ignited, and sure enough after a moment or two he raised his head, and there was a little of the old light in his eyes. 'I am, as you see, quite idle at present, and a mystery may serve to pass the time.'

'I took the liberty —' I began.

'Oh?'

'I thought you might find the mystery of some interest, so I delved into the old periodicals in the reading room and found the account of the inquest in the London papers. I expect you already have them here — somewhere —' I looked about me — 'if they could be found.'

'The gift of knowledge!' Holmes exclaimed, starting up into a sitting position. 'There is nothing better. I am indebted to you, Stamford.'

I handed him my newspapers and he busied himself with them. There was little enough to discover. The deceased was thought to be aged about fifty and was respectably though simply dressed. The tragedy had occurred during a heavy rainstorm and had been witnessed by a number of passers-by who thought the man had been rushing across the street without looking about him properly. The cab driver had shouted a warning and made every effort to pull up his horses but had not been able to do so in time, as the wooden paving was wet and slippery. The inquest had delivered a verdict of accidental death.

'He appears to have been crossing Cheapside in the direction of St Martin's Le Grand,' said Holmes. 'I know the spot; it can be a rushing river of carriages at certain times of the day, and one has to be smart on one's feet to avoid a similar fate. Of course, where he was coming from and where he was bound remain unknown.' He paused for a moment, then carefully knocked out his pipe into a saucer — which was almost overflowing with similar detritus — and rose to his feet. 'Allow me a little time to make myself presentable and I will return to Barts and examine what remains. Perhaps Danville and the doctor who attended the patient may furnish some additional facts.'

Holmes disappeared into his bedroom, and I waited for him, resisting the urge to air and tidy his room. It was my natural instinct to want to restore the books and papers to some semblance of order, but I sensed that despite appearances Holmes knew precisely where everything was. When he emerged, fully dressed and perfectly groomed, he smiled at my expression. 'It is true, Stamford; I do know where everything is. If I wanted someone to move my possessions to places where it would take me weeks to find them again, I would marry, but that I shall never do.'

At Barts we found Danville, who showed us the little box of the deceased man's effects on a shelf in the dissection room. Holmes laid the materials out on a bench with great care, almost as if he was reconstructing the man himself from a skeleton. There were few enough items — a pair of scuffed and dirty boots, a small leather coin purse, a pocket handkerchief, a pencil, and a notebook with several pages torn out, the remaining pages blank.

Holmes raised the notebook, holding the top page out to the light from the window. 'There are impressions of writing here from earlier pages,' he said. 'The most recent note appears to be composed only of numbers rather than words, but they are hard to make out. I may be able to restore them to view.'

'We hoped, because of the unusual formation of the foot, that someone would know who he was,' said Danville.

'Such a condition might not be known to friends or an employer,' said Holmes, 'only close family.' He turned his attention to the boots. 'This man prided himself on his appearance but had insufficient funds to dress as he would please. The boots were handmade by a master craftsman and would have been very expensive when new, but they were not made for him. He has had them second-hand.'

'How do you know?' asked Danville.

'If he had had them made for himself, the maker would have accommodated the additional width required for his extra toes, but he did not. Therefore, they were made for another. In order to make them more comfortable, the wearer has had them adjusted with the insertion of a small piece of leather. They have also been re-soled and re-lined, but this work was not done by so skilled a hand as the original maker, of whom no trace remains. The boots have been well and regularly cleaned; the only mud splashes I can see originated from a single location and one journey, presumably the rainy day on which the accident took place. The only marks of damage appear to be from the accident. Have any enquiries been made of bootmakers?'

'Not that I am aware of,' said Danville.

Holmes took out his magnifying glass and studied the stitching. 'Unfortunately, the repair work is some years old, and might have been done anywhere.' He opened the coin purse and laid out the contents, which was nothing more than a few shillings and copper coins. 'Was this in his pocket? I ask because it has suffered no noticeable damage.'

'It was found in an inside pocket,' said Danville.

'One of the kind protected with a flap and a button?' asked Holmes.

'I believe so. He obviously liked to keep his money very secure.'

Holmes examined the empty purse carefully, paying particular attention to the interior. 'There is a lining with something in it,' he said, 'and a gap for the fingers.' He delved into it, and with an exclamation of triumph he extracted a folded slip of paper. This he gently opened out and laid on the bench, smoothing it so it could be read. Picking up the notebook, he matched the torn edges. 'The most recent missing page,' he said. 'Black ink written with a standard J nib, if I am not mistaken.'

We stared at the note. It read simply: - *160, 2, 14, 102, 1, 52, 402, 2, 20, 253, 2, 36, 101, 2, 7, 419, 1, 9, 482, 2, 21, 415, 2, 42*

'It's just a list of numbers,' said Danville. 'What do you think they mean? An inventory of goods, perhaps? Or a list of debts for his employer?'

'Perhaps,' said Holmes. He made an exact note of the numbers in his pocketbook before folding the paper and returning it to its secret location. Once this was done, the sad remains of an unknown life were replaced in the box. 'Do not dispose of these,' said Holmes. 'I will make some enquiries and see if I can discover the identity of the owner. Someone somewhere must be missing this man.'

CHAPTER TWO

Mr Edwards, the house surgeon who had attended the patient, had nothing to tell us. His main contribution to the incident had been to certify death. Nurse Harmon was more helpful. The nurses at Barts are, in my opinion, amongst the best in the world. Impeccably uniformed, efficient, and sympathetic, they inspire the confidence of patients with their calm yet comforting presence. Nurse Harmon, a person of quiet yet formidable talent, was the epitome of the perfect nurse, strong yet gentle, and wedded devotedly to her work. Some of the medical students comment on the nurses only for their beauty or lack of it, a practice I deplore as disrespectful. I would have been proud for any sister of mine to enter that profession.

Nurse Harmon told us that when the unknown man had been brought in, he was very clearly in a dying state. The wheels of the cab had passed across his chest and abdomen, causing numerous fractures to his ribs, and inevitably, fatal injuries to the underlying organs. The hoof of one of the horses had broken his jaw and cheekbone. Unable to speak, he had been in great pain and distress, and nothing could be done for him except to ease his sufferings. His few possessions had been placed by his bedside and he had cast anxious glances at them and attempted to gesture at his coin purse. Assuming that he was concerned for the money it contained, Nurse Harmon had told him that she would keep it safe, but that had not seemed to reassure him. He had died shortly afterwards. The only useful clue to his identity was therefore the paper he had carried, and I could see that Holmes was determined to extract its mysteries.

I recalled Holmes once mentioning to me that he had uncovered a coded meaning in a message directed to the father of a college friend. 'You are right, Stamford,' he said, when I referred to it. 'This looks to me like a kind of code, but a very different one from the one I encountered earlier, which was simple in the extreme. I have made a study of the art of secret writing, which you may be surprised to know goes back to ancient times. In one of its most basic forms, a letter of the alphabet may be substituted by another letter or a number or a symbol. It requires both the sender and recipient to have a code book with the key. But that is easily solved, since letters are used with known frequencies and I daresay I could read any such code without any difficulty, especially in the English language. From time to time I see coded messages in the advertisements of the daily newspapers, and I have amused myself by solving them. The results, however, have been extremely unedifying.'

'Do you think this a code of that kind?' I asked.

'No. To my mind, the selection of numbers suggests that it refers not to letters of the alphabet but to words to be found in the pages of a book. If you look at the arrangement of numbers, what do you see?'

I studied them carefully. 'There are a lot of ones and twos,' I said.

'More precisely we have a long number, followed by either a one or a two followed by a number no greater than fifty-two.' I was still looking mystified, so he smiled and went on. 'Consider, Stamford, if you wished to send a message composed of words picked out of a book, and did not want to search through its pages, a set of Dickens or a bible, for example, to find the exact word you required, what would be the best kind of book to use?'

I could see his point. How would I guarantee that any word I wanted for my message would be included? How would I find it quickly? 'Oh, of course, a dictionary!'

'Well done! It is my belief that the numbers in this message may be seen as groups of three. The first is the number of the page, showing that the volume has at the very least 482 pages; the second, which is either one or two, refers I think to the column. Many dictionaries are laid out in double columns. The third number points us to the word entered in that column.'

'It is a very short message,' I said. 'Just eight words.'

'The answer may of course be of no interest at all. A missive between lovers, an assignation, fear of discovery or some such. I have the feeling that our man was not the sender but merely the messenger. And judging by the pages missing from his notebook, it was a task he had been trusted to carry out before.'

'Do you know which book was used?' I asked.

'That, of course, is the difficulty. There are many dictionaries, and they can run to several editions. The wrong one would result only in nonsense. But I believe I now have a field to explore, and we shall see if I can achieve a result.'

I didn't see Holmes for several days after that conversation, and I guessed that he was at the British Museum Library scouring every dictionary or work of reference they had. It might have seemed an onerous pastime to some, but I think in a curious way Holmes derived pleasure from such quiet, painstaking, solitary study.

When I next saw him, I was expecting to learn that the message concerned some frivolous or even vulgar adventure, but his expression was severe.

'I have my answer, but it was not what I was expecting,' he said. 'The volume concerned was a British edition of Webster's some twenty years old. Nothing else gave a result. The message reads: "Four dead suspect murder danger to you three".'

'How extraordinary!' I exclaimed. 'And a serious matter, if it means what it appears to mean. Surely no-one would joke or play a prank in that way.'

'As it stands, it is a dire warning of a threat to life,' said Holmes. 'And importantly, a warning which never reached its intended recipient, whoever that might be. I fear that we may have intercepted a disagreement within a gang of criminals or even spies. Such desperate characters would not hesitate to destroy any one of their number who they thought might betray them. But who are the four dead? Who is the suspected murderer? Who are the three in danger?'

'Ummm,' I began hesitantly. He looked at me. 'Maybe the police have already been looking for this gang and know about the messages?' I suggested.

'I understand you, but no. I did consult Sergeant Lestrade, who is the least dull in the force I have been privileged to meet, and he assures me that this is all new to him and he has no knowledge of any such gang or their messages, or indeed of any incident where four people have died from apparent criminal activity. There have been murders and unexplained deaths in recent months which may be involved, but at present there is no means of connecting them, if connections there be.'

'Then there is nothing to be done,' I said.

'We keep our wits about us, our eyes and ears open, and we wait,' said Holmes. 'In the meantime, I will examine the newspapers for reports of deaths in the few months before this accident, which might be the ones referred to in the message. The writer of the note states that he only suspects murder, so most likely the deaths may not yet have been determined to be the result of crime.'

This was an endeavour in which I thought I could be of assistance, especially as several recent deaths following accidents had taken place in the hospital and the inquests had been held there. As I began my self-imposed task, I realised that I had no idea of the type of incident Holmes was looking for, and I suspected neither did he. His taste, however, was always for the outré, and he despised the purely commonplace which he thought beneath his notice, so I decided to look for reports which would capture his attention. As I perused the papers held in the Abernethian room, I saw the usual deaths one might expect in the normal course of the world's ways: consumption, malnutrition, a drunken plunge from a railway bridge, colliery explosions and lead poisoning amongst factory workers. None of the inquests examined the related deaths of four persons. The four deaths in the message could therefore have occurred on up to four separate occasions.

Many fatalities were the result of negligence, foolish behaviour, and plain bad luck. Two workmen had been killed while sheltering from a violent thunderstorm under a brick archway which had collapsed after nine tons of builder's ballast had been unloaded on top of it.

The wife of a carpenter, and mother of five children, had been extremely unfortunate to be shot in the head by a ricochet from a rifle gallery at the Alexandra Palace pleasure park during a family visit.

An art dealer had, probably from curiosity, wandered too close to the burnt out remains of a warehouse fire, only to have a floor give way underneath him, plunging him into the basement.

A young labourer, engaging in horseplay with his friends in which a wager had been involved, had been tied to a cat and pushed into a river. The cat had survived but the man had drowned.

At St George's Hospital the iron water tank on the roof had burst, and part of the tank and its contents had descended through the ceiling. A bedridden patient and her bed were later found in another ward, two floors below.

Other deaths were perhaps more mysterious or had additional features of interest. An itinerant with a wooden leg had been dragged below a hurrying brougham conveying a Member of Parliament, and there was the unaccountable suicide of a Prussian barrister whose body had been found floating in the Thames.

I presented my results to Holmes, who, if he was pleased by my endeavours on his behalf, managed to conceal the depth of his gratitude.

A week later I was assisting Holmes with one of his mysterious chemistry experiments, when Nurse Harmon entered the laboratory. 'I am sorry to interrupt you, gentlemen,' she began, 'but I thought you might like to know that the man with the two extra toes has been identified. His sister has come.'

Holmes was instantly all attention. 'Is she still here?' he asked.

'She is. I have put her in the nurse's office as she is rather upset. She is a Mrs Crowder from Norfolk.'

'I will speak to her,' said Holmes. 'There is still much to be learned.'

He lost no time in sweeping from the room, and I decided to go with him.

The bereaved woman, a matronly figure in country clothes, who had been provided with a glass of water, was sitting disconsolately in a corner, holding her brother's leather boots in her arms as if they had been her twin infants.

'Mrs Crowder,' said Holmes, in an uncharacteristically sympathetic tone.

She looked up.

'With your permission, I would like to ask you some questions about your brother.'

She uttered a deep, soulful sigh. 'He was a good man, sir.'

Holmes took this statement as assent and pulled up a chair beside her. 'What was his name and profession?'

'Charlie Wilson. He was in service. I mean, he was like a senior man, supervising others. He worked at the boys' day school, St John's Academy in Noble Street.'

'I suppose I don't need to ask if you can identify his possessions.'

She ran her fingertips over the right boot where the leather had been extended to accommodate the additional toes. 'Oh, I know this is his. He had seven toes on his right foot.'

'When did you last see him?'

'In the summer. He came to stay with us for a week. We used to write as well, quite often. Family news and suchlike.'

'And what brought you to London? Was it to see him?'

'Yes. I don't come to London much. It's too big for me. But — about two or three weeks ago, I had a letter from a solicitor. Our aunt had died and left us some money. Charlie was due to get £25. I wrote to him, but he didn't write back. I was worried. It wasn't like him not to write. I thought he might be ill.'

'And what did you learn of him?'

'The first place I went to was the school, as I thought he would be there in the day, but Mr Bradstreet — the headmaster — said that Charlie didn't work there anymore,

22

that he had found another position that suited him better and had gone away. But he couldn't tell me where. So I went to Charlie's lodgings.' Her voice faltered. 'The landlady — she was a slatternly sort, not the kind to trouble herself. She told me he had gone away without notice a month ago. She had sold his belongings — she said it was her right — it was in place of the rent she ought to have had — and she had let the rooms to someone else.'

'Did your brother own any books?' asked Holmes.

Mrs Crowder, her lips trembling, was too sunk in her own misery to consider whether this was a strange question. 'Just the one, sir, the Holy Bible. It was a family bible, and I went round all the second-hand bookshops looking for it, but I didn't find it.' She drew a sleeve across her eyes.

'And what brought you here?'

'I thought to ask about if anyone had seen Charlie, and then someone remembered hearing about the man run over by a cab and taken here. It was in the London newspapers. When I heard he had a foot with seven toes, I knew it couldn't be anyone else.'

'This purse is his?' asked Holmes, picking up that item.

'Yes, sir.'

'Do you know that there is a paper in it with some writing?'

'A paper? No. Only a few coins.'

Holmes opened the purse, took the paper slip from its hiding place, opened it out, and showed it to her. 'Does this mean anything to you?'

'No.'

'Is it your brother's writing?'

She looked at it for a few moments then shook her head. 'No. It's just numbers, but — he never made his numbers like that. He didn't write this.'

'He must have been carrying a message for someone,' said Holmes. 'Do you mind if I keep this?'

'No,' she said.

Nurse Harmon returned to see how Mrs Crowder did. 'I'll help you wrap the things to take away,' she said kindly, 'and then we'll see about getting your brother's death properly registered, and I can show you where he is buried.'

As the nurse conducted the grieving sister from the room, Holmes slipped the paper note between the pages of his pocketbook. 'Mr Bradstreet the headmaster was curiously unhelpful to Mrs Crowder,' he observed. 'I think he may know more than he was willing to say. Let us pay him a visit.'

CHAPTER THREE

In Noble Street, a confident businessman had once constructed a handsome townhouse to demonstrate his solid success but had later sensibly decided to decamp to a leafier location. The building remained, a little careworn and less handsome, and had been converted to be used as a boys' school.

Noble Street was a relatively quiet backwater near to the commercial bustle of Gresham Street with its many giant warehouses and lumbering goods wagons. Quite recently, a three-storey furniture warehouse had been ravaged by a fire which had blazed for two days and destroyed both the building and its contents. Several firemen and incautious sightseers had been injured by falling masonry and taken to Barts. The art dealer whose death had been reported in the newspapers had suffered his deadly fall at the smouldering site and lingered painfully in hospital for some days before he'd expired. Demolition of the remaining brickwork to make the area safe was in cautious progress, but as Holmes and I made our way to the school, I was relieved not to have to pass close to the still perilously unstable ruin where there remained a stinging odour of burnt wood, paint, and varnish.

The door was answered by an elderly manservant, and Holmes was obliged to explain that we had come from St Bartholomew's Hospital to speak to the headmaster concerning his former employee, Charles Wilson. We were invited in and told to wait in the hallway. Those pupils and masters who passed along on their way to classes showed that the school catered not for the sons of the fashionable elite, but for the great mass of London boys whose parents hoped they might advance themselves through education. It reminded me of my own schooldays.

Holmes glanced around him, and I saw his nostrils twitch. 'Damp,' he said. 'There are some pails rather poorly hidden at the end of the corridor. I would not care to be in here when it rains.' Fortunately, we were not required to wait long before we were admitted to the study of the headmaster, Mr Bradstreet.

Bradstreet was rather more youthful than I had expected, perhaps in his early thirties. When he rose in greeting, gesturing us to seats that faced his desk, I saw he was a tall, broad fellow, though with the incipient jowls which were the harbingers of middle-aged portliness. Boys' schools usually emphasise the character building and health benefits of team sports, and it was obvious that Mr Bradstreet embraced this ideal. There were shelves behind his desk displaying silver sporting trophies, some of which were topped with the shape of a rugby football, and the walls were hung with framed certificates, all with a sporting theme. An oar and a cricket bat, both of which were marked with use, were leaning in one corner.

Despite his friendliness, which appeared a little forced, I sensed that the nature of our errand troubled him.

'I was told that you had come from Barts Hospital with some news,' he said, taking his seat once more.

'We have,' said Holmes smoothly. I wondered if Bradstreet thought we were young surgeons, and Holmes obviously saw no reason to alter that impression. 'You may recall some weeks ago the newspapers carried a report of an unidentified man who was killed after being run over by a cab not far from here, and who died at the hospital. He has now been identified by his sister as Charles Wilson, who was once employed by this school.'

Bradstreet looked unsettled by the news. I saw his fingers tapping on the desktop, then the letter he had been writing was pushed aside to enable him to lean forward, his hands placed flat on the desk as if needing its support. 'I am sorry to hear it,' he said at last. 'He was a good employee, diligent, well-mannered, trustworthy. He supervised the building and the junior servants. Is there anything I can do to assist you or the family?'

'You informed his sister that he had left for another position,' said Holmes. 'I am trying to find his most recent employer.'

'Yes, it must have been only a few days before that terrible accident. He told me he had found a situation that suited him better, but he did not say where. I gave him a good character and wished him well.'

'Did you go to Barts to try and identify the body?'

Bradstreet looked quite unnerved by the question and took a little while to formulate his reply. 'I — I confess I did — I thought it my public duty to do so — but it was a dreadful sight, and I could not in all honesty say that it was he. I felt quite unwell and thought I might faint, so I came away.'

Holmes looked at him severely, then he abruptly started to his feet and walked around the desk.

Bradstreet reeled back at the sudden movement. 'What are you doing?' he demanded.

Holmes said nothing but picked up the letter the headmaster had started to write. The body of the letter, which was on notepaper printed with the name and address of the school, had got little further than the date and the opening greeting, but nevertheless Holmes gave it his detailed attention. Then he placed it on the desk, took out his magnifying glass and studied it. I was used to Holmes' methods, of course, but Bradstreet could only stare in astonishment.

Straightening up to his full height, Holmes said, 'You have a very characteristic way of making your figures, Mr Bradstreet. I see a long horizontal on the number four, also a little hook on the one.'

'What of it?'

'I have seen this style before very recently.' Holmes took from his pocket the little folded slip with the message which Wilson had had hidden in his coin purse. 'You wrote this, did you not?'

Bradstreet went pale with shock. 'Where did you get that?'

'The unfortunate Mr Wilson had it hidden about his person. I believe you have lied to both his sister and to us. He never left your employ, did he? I believe that you wrote this message and asked him to deliver it for you. When he did not return, you feared that the man killed in the accident might be Mr Wilson, and you went to Barts not to identify the body but to reassure yourself that he was coming back from his mission, and the message was not amongst his possessions and had therefore been delivered. But you were unaware of how well he had kept it hidden. You must have suspected that the dead man was Wilson from his clothing. Why did you say nothing?'

Bradstreet began to tremble. 'I could not be sure it was he,' he said, 'and even if I had been, I had no knowledge of his family, so there was no-one I could inform. I assumed they would read his description in the newspapers and come forward.'

'And now, of course,' said Holmes, relentlessly, 'you must realise that your message never reached its intended recipient. I assume that Wilson was unable to find the individual and was returning to advise you of this when he met his end. Who was the message for, Mr Bradstreet? And more importantly, who are the four dead?'

I have never seen a man so aghast, so bewildered as the headmaster was then. 'How did you…' He broke off.

'It was not difficult,' said Holmes, airily. 'I see you have a twenty-year-old British edition of Webster's on your bookshelf. That was all I needed to know.'

Bradstreet gulped and stood up so quickly that his chair rocked back on its legs. 'I need — I need to go out,' he gasped. 'I must go at once. It is a matter of life and death!'

CHAPTER FOUR

The headmaster wasted no time but went to a coat stand where his greatcoat and hat were hanging. As he took the heavy coat down, I saw him wince with the effort and it was apparent that he had some difficulty putting on the garment. 'Old sporting injury,' he commented by way of explanation, as Holmes took it upon himself to help him on with the coat.

'I'll accompany you,' said Holmes.

'If you wouldn't mind,' said Bradstreet, 'it would go better if I went alone. It isn't far, and I promise you I will be back very soon. I also think in view of what you already know, I had better tell you all. But that can wait until I return. If you would be kind enough to wait for me here? I'll tell my man you can remain.'

Holmes agreed and Bradstreet donned his hat, took a walking cane, and left in a hurry.

'Stamford,' said Holmes, grimly, 'follow him, but make sure you are not seen. Observe where he goes and to whom he speaks. See if any messages are passed. Then come back before he returns. I will look for any further clues that might be here.'

This was not at all how I had expected the day to proceed, but as anyone might when issued with such a peremptory order by Sherlock Holmes, I jumped to it and obeyed.

I did wonder in view of the desperate rush whether Bradstreet would summon a cab, in which case I might be in some difficulty, but he showed no sign of doing so. In the London thoroughfares crowded with cabs and carriages, it was often far quicker to make a short and unencumbered journey on foot. Avoiding the narrow alleyway of Foster Lane, which was packed with surging humanity, Bradstreet turned right into Gresham Street before taking the wider way of St Martin's Le Grand where he could walk more freely, and then turned south towards Cheapside. Here he wove his way through the commercial bustle of men with important business, the darting, swerving messenger boys whose business was measured in minutes and pennies, and the idlers, who had no business at all. For one moment I wondered if I was not the only person following Bradstreet, as I heard some rapidly padding footsteps behind me, then I glanced around and saw a snub-nosed street boy who was obviously hot on some other errand. He dashed past me and past Bradstreet too and hurried on.

I realised as I followed the headmaster that he was approaching the location of the unfortunate Mr Wilson's accident. I was half expecting him to enter one of the many shops or inns in that area but instead, to my great surprise, I saw him enter Canon Alley, striding past the taverns, booksellers, and bookbinders, and before I knew it, I was following him up the steps of the north entrance to St Paul's Cathedral.

Here, he stopped and looked about him. I was obliged to conceal myself behind a column, where I pretended to be studying the architecture very carefully without of course taking my attention from Bradstreet. After a while, he approached one of the guides, and seemed to be asking him some questions in a very earnest manner. The man listened and nodded, then it was apparent from his gestures that Bradstreet was to remain where he was while he went to make some enquiries for him. He moved away, and Bradstreet sat in one of the chairs facing the high altar, folded his hands in his lap and waited impatiently. After a moment or two, he bowed his head and I suspected that he was praying. Several minutes passed, then the guide returned, and there was a conversation. Whatever was being communicated it was not good news, but neither was it disastrous. Bradstreet nodded despondently, and the guide returned to his duties.

I expected Bradstreet to return to the school, but he stood for a while, sighing and indecisive. Then something attracted his attention. He looked up. I followed his gaze and I saw something high above, a figure standing at the railings of the famous whispering gallery, not so close that I could make out any details, but with an arm extended, and there was a colourful movement of something like a handkerchief. At this, Bradstreet's whole demeanour changed. He appeared greatly relieved and heartened at the sight. I saw his lips move. I could not hear what he was saying, but he appeared to be uttering a prayer of thanks. Moved to action, he hurried to the steps which led to the gallery. I emerged from my concealment in the shelter of the column but decided not to follow him, as I felt sure I would be seen. The flutter of colour had gone by now, but there was undoubtedly someone still up there, and it was obvious to me that Bradstreet had gone to meet them. I decided to wait until the meeting was over and they descended so I could at the very least describe this individual to Holmes.

Once Bradstreet was above me his height meant that he was easily visible in the gallery, although his companion, lurking behind him nearer to the wall, was not. After some conversation between the two, Bradstreet approached the railings and appeared to be staring into the distance, craning his neck, and looking for something that was being pointed out to him. He lifted one hand from the railing to gesture. Then, without warning, he launched himself into the air.

The scream when it came was like nothing I had ever heard before. A high grinding sound of desperation, torn from a male throat. For a moment I was unaware of anyone around me, though of course there were many others, but in that second it was just myself and the man. Bradstreet was above me with his arms spread out and his greatcoat open like the wings of a bat. Then the wings folded, and he plummeted down.

A thousand thoughts can pass though the mind in moments. One can see a tragedy about to happen and yet despite everything, despite the inevitability of it all, there is a brief hope that somehow it can be averted, or the blow softened. Would there perhaps be something to break that terrible fall? If there was, could the man live? There were rows of wooden chairs laid out on the floor below, and Bradstreet, wide-eyed and screaming, crashed on top of them, the weight of his body crushing the frames and splintering the wood. Then the broken leg of a chair ran like a spear through his body, impaling him in a burst of blood, and he lay still.

There were shrieks all around me. I moved forward to see if there was anything I could do, but one of the guides, looking a little green about the face, began urging visitors to stay calm and leave as quickly as possible. Those gentlemen with lady companions were already bound for the exit, although a few curiosity seekers were trying to view the horrible wreckage. I tried to explain that I was a medical student and might be able to help, but my voice was lost in the general hubbub. With others I was urged towards the nearest door. It was obvious, however, that the man must be dead. I looked back towards the whispering gallery. Some of the vergers had appeared and were leaning on the railings, staring down at the tragedy. I thought that whoever it was Bradstreet had gone to see must have descended in the confusion and might even now be mingling with the crowd making their way from the building. Then I was jostled down the steps towards Canon Alley, where

I stood for a few moments, gasping in the chill air. I had seen death many times before, of course, but never so sudden or shocking as this, and that of a man in good health with whom I had been conversing only minutes before.

All I could do was return to the school and tell Holmes what had occurred.

When I arrived, he took one look at me, directed me to a chair and poured a glass of water from a carafe. He knew the importance of obtaining my account as soon as possible while every detail was fresh in my mind, and he questioned me closely. I gave my answers between noisy spluttering gulps. What colour was the waving fabric? I guessed at mustard yellow. Was the person who Bradstreet met male or female? I had the impression from what I had seen of the coat sleeve that it was a male. Did I see Bradstreet climb the railings? No, it was as if he had launched himself forward like a man diving into water. Did I see anyone at all behaving in a suspicious manner? No.

'Since you were there with the express purpose of observing Bradstreet, you most probably saw more of what occurred than anyone else,' said Holmes. 'You must give a full statement to the police at once.'

'The police?' I queried.

'I think it very likely that you have just witnessed a murder.'

CHAPTER FIVE

Pausing only to tell the servant that the headmaster had met with an accident at the cathedral and would not be returning, we hurried to St Paul's, where we were sure that the City of London Police would already have been summoned. Holmes commented that if the men of the far larger Metropolitan Police should arrive as well, it would suggest that a wider ranging investigation was thought necessary, but he thought it unlikely at this stage. 'The two forces are not rivals as many suggest, but cohorts,' he said. 'All the same, they like to police their own areas as far as they can.'

As we made our way, Holmes told me that his examination of the headmaster's study had borne little fruit. 'His papers were not excessive and very tidily and methodically arranged. I know many men of business are in the habit of burning old correspondence, and I sense that Bradstreet was such a man. It is a habit applauded by maidservants but deplored by anyone wishing to learn something of the individual concerned. I saw no evidence of grinding penury or debt, but certainly none of luxury. The school, as so many of this type do, exists in constant need of funds, and particularly so at present, as I observed when I arrived that repairs to the building are long overdue. The trophies on display were silver plate and donated by proud parents. The certificates of sporting prowess and the cricket bat and oar related to Bradstreet's college days.'

'On such a brief acquaintance, he seemed a very dedicated and inoffensive fellow,' I observed. 'Who would want to murder him?'

'One cannot entirely rule out the work of a madman,' said Holmes, drily, 'but in view of his undelivered message, one possible explanation is that he was killed to prevent his passing on information which would have been very damaging to a dangerous person. Everything in his manner suggested that he was in fear — if not for his own life than for that of another. How such a man became embroiled in a circumstance of that nature is a mystery.'

News of the tragedy had spread and the open spaces outside the cathedral were crowded with onlookers, many of whom had left their usual businesses and perambulations to join the prattling throng. Amongst the hubbub of uninformed speculation, we overheard those who had been inside the building when the headmaster fell being eagerly quizzed by recent arrivals. It was apparent that none of those questioned had seen more than the culmination of the fall, having first been alerted by the hideous scream. A surgeon had been seen entering the cathedral to view the body, and it was assumed that he would experience no difficulty in pronouncing life extinct. The remains of the unfortunate headmaster had yet to be removed.

The police were much in evidence, circulating through the crowds, ensuring that no unauthorised person was permitted to enter the cathedral, and dismissing anyone they recognised as a pickpocket drawn to the crush by opportunity. They were also asking for witnesses and interviewing anyone who had information. When my turn came, I described what I had seen and provided my address. I felt sure I would be called to give evidence at the inquest. The constable to whom I spoke was sufficiently interested in my account to alert an inspector to whom I repeated my tale. Inspector Hardiman was a youthful fellow with bright buttons, a luxuriant moustache, and a serious expression. He listened with great care, noting our suspicions, also the fact that Sergeant Lestrade of the Metropolitan Police had previously been advised of the headmaster's message before we knew the identity of the sender. He confirmed that the body would be taken to Barts for a post-mortem examination, and the inquest held there, and advised me that the secret code and its import should not be mentioned in court, as this was a detail he would prefer for the moment not to be reported in the press. I was somewhat relieved at that. If, as Holmes suspected, Bradstreet had been killed because of something he knew, revealing that we too knew the contents of the message might make us similar targets.

Holmes had been eager to examine the two crucial sites; the position in which Bradstreet had been standing in the gallery, and where he had landed, but the cathedral entrances were guarded by police and his intention was frustrated. Holmes the twenty-two-year-old student was not yet the man whom Watson was to know in years to come, the lauded professional detective, frequently consulted by the police on their most difficult cases, who was easily able to brush aside any official barriers to his work. He grumbled that we would have to return once the area was clear of hindrances but questioned me in detail concerning the exact location of the crushed and bloody chairs, and the point where the headmaster's deadly dive had begun.

'Bradstreet was a large, heavy man,' I observed. 'It must have been a very hard task to push him over the railings with any prospect of success. I don't recall seeing anyone in the cathedral of greater height than he, or uncommonly powerful.'

'That is true,' agreed Holmes, 'but if I am correct in my suspicions,' he added, in that tone he was wont to adopt when the word 'if' was merely a polite embellishment, 'Bradstreet was killed not only by someone he knew and trusted, but someone who knew his history well enough to have precise knowledge of his injury and make use of it.'

On the following day the inquest concerning the death of Frank Bradstreet, headmaster, aged thirty-two, was opened by the City of London coroner Mr William Payne in the rather drab stewards' room at Barts. A fire flickered fitfully in the grate, offering little comfort to the stuffy air which, despite the best efforts of the hospital servants, always seemed to smell of dust and decay. The jurymen had had the dubious privilege of viewing the shattered body before the proceedings began and judging by their expressions when they took their seats, they had not been uplifted by the experience.

I saw Inspector Hardiman in attendance, and he was joined by Sergeant Lestrade. The two policemen conferred at length in voices too quiet to be overheard. At one point, Lestrade made a comment which led to raised eyebrows and Hardiman sent a rapid astonished glance in our direction.

In the event, the only evidence taken was confirmation of the identity of the deceased, and the hearing was adjourned for the post-mortem examination to be completed. Holmes was impatient to return to St Paul's, where he anticipated having more freedom of action than he'd had on the previous day, and as principal witness to the death my presence was imperative.

Any visitor to the cathedral that afternoon would have been hard-pressed to imagine that such a gruesome tragedy had occurred so recently. The police had gone, the damaged chairs removed, and the floor carefully cleansed of blood. There was a large number of visitors, some of whom, I felt, had come less to admire the architecture or say their prayers, than to stare at the place where a man had plunged to a horrible death. I saw enough people pointing up at the gallery and then imagining the dreadful fall with the movement of their eyes. Their interest was all too obvious, and they attracted stares of disapproval from the religious patrons and dedicated staff. I guessed that Holmes and I would not look out of place amongst the gazing curious, but all the same I felt a little embarrassed by the requirement to point out under Holmes' questioning the place from which the man had fallen and where he had landed.

Holmes walked about the area, staring above him from different locations, standing first directly below the railings then moving to the place where the impact had been. He was absorbed in his task, all his mind bent to the problem, apparently oblivious to the hard looks or judgement of those around him.

'You said that just before he fell, Bradstreet was gesturing to something?'

'Yes.'

'With which hand?'

I did my best to paint the picture in my mind. 'The right one.'

'His good arm. He might have had some difficulty in extending the other one.'

'But I couldn't see what it was he was indicating.'

'Was he pointing directly down to the floor below, as if to an individual? Or was it further away?'

'Only slightly downwards, I think, as if to someone standing there or some object, but it would have been at a distance, not immediately below.'

'He had to crane his neck forward to look?'

'Yes. Whatever it was, I don't think it was easy for him to see.'

Holmes considered this, stroking his chin in thought. 'There is one other question I have yet to address fully, and this may be the key to the solution. As we know, Bradstreet's visit here was a sudden unplanned impulse, and if he was killed, and I believe he was most likely killed by someone he knew well, how did his killer happen to be here waiting for him when he arrived?'

'I suppose it could have been a coincidence, and he simply took his chance,' I suggested, but I could see from his expression that Holmes had already considered and rejected that idea, which now I had put it forward sounded weak, even to me.

'Let us go up to the gallery,' he said.

We made our way up the stairs and ventured onto the curving walkway. I must admit I was a little nervous, but I could see that Holmes, who seemed to have no nerves at all, was using his greater height to estimate how Bradstreet might have towered above the top of the railings. 'What was Bradstreet pointing to?' he asked. It was a rhetorical question and he answered it at once. 'My conclusion is — nothing at all. It is not an easy thing to simply push a man over these railings, even when such an action is unexpected, but the task was made easier because of the weakness of one arm, which the killer must have known about. He suggested to Bradstreet that there was something below that ought to attract his attention, the presence of a friend, perhaps, and inveigled him into releasing his good hand from the railing. Then he seized the man by the ankles and quickly, before he could regain his grip, tipped him over. It needed bodily strength, speed, and resolve. It was the work of a man, and a strong and desperate man at that. With all attention on the corpse, the killer was able to slip away unnoticed.'

Holmes was leaning over the railings and for one moment of sheer cold terror I almost grasped his arm to prevent an accident.

'You see the position where Bradstreet landed?' he asked. 'I regret my ignorance of higher mathematics which might have proved that he could not have reached that location without some forceful assistance from another person, or his own determination to jump. But at any rate, I feel I have to my own satisfaction ruled out any idea of an accidental fall. As to his killer, I think the man was already here before Bradstreet arrived, quite possibly because he had business here or was employed here.'

'What do you propose to do, Holmes?'

'At this moment, all I can do is write to the coroner and Inspector Hardiman with my conclusions. But I am far from being the only amateur theorist in England, and my letter will only be one of many sent to Mr Payne or the police. My views may well be ignored, and if they are, I fear that a killer will go free.'

CHAPTER SIX

Two days later the resumed inquest hearing opened with the medical evidence, which was given by house-surgeon Edwards, who had examined the deceased on admission. He stated that the body was that of a well-nourished man in good health, who had been wearing a leather brace to support his left shoulder joint, evidence of an old injury. The post-mortem examination at which he had assisted confirmed that the headmaster was not at the time of death under the influence of alcohol or a soporific drug. The deceased was not, as far as could be determined, using any form of medication, apart from the occasional application of a liniment which had no part to play in the fatality. The cause of death was without doubt the fall from a height, which had resulted in multiple serious injuries.

I was called to give evidence, and resolved to keep my account simple, direct, and truthful, answering only those questions I had been asked. I stated that I was a student of surgery at Barts Medical College. I had never met Bradstreet before the day of his death and had gone to see him to inform him that the body of a servant employed by the school, who had suffered a serious accident and died at Barts, had just been identified. When questioned concerning the headmaster's state of mind, I said that he had been very sorry to hear of the servant's death. I was pressed for more detail by the coroner, who asked why Bradstreet had suddenly left his desk in the middle of the day to go to the cathedral. I replied that he had been concerned to realise that an important message carried by his late servant had not been delivered and he had hurried away with the intention of rectifying the situation. The headmaster, I made it clear, had not revealed to me either the contents of the message or to whom it was addressed. Explaining why I had followed him to the cathedral was a more difficult exercise. I said I had done so in case he required assistance, because he had appeared agitated, and I was also aware when I saw him struggling to put on his coat that he was in pain. He had mentioned to me that this was the result of a sporting injury.

The coroner and the men of the jury listened very carefully to my account of the individual with the yellow handkerchief whom Bradstreet had appeared to recognise and the unexpected plunge that had followed, but whether they, like Holmes, had formed the suspicion that the headmaster had been murdered I could not say. I returned to my seat with some relief, especially when Holmes gave a brief nod of approval.

Mr Jarvis, the cathedral guide whom I had seen speaking to Bradstreet, was next called to give evidence. He answered the coroner's questions with all the confidence of a man used to making pronouncements to an interested assembly. 'I had spoken to the gentleman before,' he said. 'He struck me as a nervous sort of person. About a month ago he came to St Paul's asking about a friend of his, a Mr Geeson who works in the cathedral library. He said that he had sent him an urgent message but had received no response and was worried in case Geeson was indisposed. I reassured him, saying that as far as I knew Geeson was perfectly well, but he had had to depart London very suddenly on being informed of a circumstance concerning his family, who reside in Lincolnshire, which required his immediate presence. It was a private matter, and he supplied no further information. Mr Bradstreet gave me his card and asked to be informed at once should Geeson return.'

'And what was the nature of his second enquiry?' asked the coroner.

'Again, he was asking about Geeson. He wanted to know if his friend had returned to his duties. I went to the library and asked, but I was told they had received another letter from Geeson to inform them that he was still having to deal with family matters which were very complicated and would require an extended leave of absence. I went back to the gentleman and told him what I had learned.'

'What was his state of mind when you gave him this news?'

Jarvis took a deep, thoughtful breath. 'It was hard to tell. He was clearly unhappy at not seeing his friend, but he appeared to accept the situation. He was not overly distressed by it.'

'Did he reveal the nature of the urgent message?'

'No, he did not.'

'Did you see him go up to the gallery?'

'No, I had to leave him alone at that time, as I was about to take a party of visitors on a tour of the vaults. There was nothing in his manner which suggested to me that he was contemplating any desperate action.'

'Can you tell the court the height of the whispering gallery?'

Jarvis, who had undoubtedly been asked this question many times, replied without hesitation, 'Yes, from the ground floor to the top of the railings it is one hundred and one feet.'

'From the ground floor, how easy is it to see who is on the gallery?'

'I would say — if the person is leaning on the railings, one could see them, but if standing further back, that is harder.'

'What is the height of the railing?'

'Four feet and two inches.'

'It would be hard for anyone to simply fall from the gallery?'

'Even a tall man such as he was, could not, I think, tumble over by accident. This has never happened to my knowledge.'

'He might have been able to climb over the railings?'

'He might, yes, if he had it in his mind to do so. One cannot guard against that, of course.'

'Did you see another person on the whispering gallery at that time?'

'I did not especially look. I don't recall seeing someone with a colourful handkerchief.' That was the end of Jarvis's testimony.

The coroner then produced a document from his bundle of papers and informed us that a Miss Margaret Ellison, the headmaster's betrothed, who was too unwell to attend in person had provided a statement which he would proceed to read out to the court. The formal tones of a man in his fifties did little to conjure up a picture of the grieving maiden who had penned the words. 'I have known Frank Bradstreet for eight years. For the last four we have been engaged to be married. He is the kindest and best natured of men, whose only wish was to be useful to society. He wanted to wait until his investments had matured before we married so he could provide me with every possible comfort. He told me he had excellent prospects. He had been despondent recently, which was out of his usual character. He said it was because of the recent death of a good friend of his called Scordell, who suffered a fall at the location of the recent fire in Gresham Street.'

I glanced at Holmes, whose interest had been instantly alerted. Both of us had recognised one of the singular deaths I had noted from the newspapers. Several men had been injured at that fire and its aftermath, but only one had died following an accident at the site. Was this friend of Bradstreet's, Mr

Scordell, one of the four dead mentioned in the warning message?

The next witness was a gentleman aged about sixty, attired in deep mourning. I have of course seen many recently bereaved persons at the hospital who have come to make the final arrangements for their loved ones, and I recognised in his strong upright bearing the iron will to do what was right and necessary even under the crushing weight of grief.

When asked for his details, he replied in a firm voice that hardly faltered at all, 'My name is Andrew Bradstreet. I am a retired schoolmaster. I am the father of Frank Bradstreet. I want to tell the court something about my son, so there can be no doubts as to his character. Our family has always been respectable and devoted to academic study and the instruction of the young. My father was a schoolmaster before me. Frank, through diligent application and the gift of an excellent memory, was able to get a scholarship to university, where he obtained his degree and also took part in college sports. He went on to teach before being offered a post as headmaster of St John's Academy, where he earned the approbation and gratitude of the parents.'

'Mr Bradstreet,' said the coroner in a sympathetic tone, after listening carefully to the bereaved father's tribute, 'it is important that the court should be advised of any circumstances you are aware of which might have led to this tragedy. Please tell us everything that you think could assist the jury in reaching a proper verdict.'

'I understand,' said Bradstreet. 'It is my belief that what occurred can only have been an accident. I have heard what the previous witnesses have said, but there is a circumstance which I need to elaborate upon. About two years ago, my son suffered an extremely serious injury while playing rugby football. He dislocated his left shoulder. Although the joint was restored under surgery, he was unable to make a full recovery and as a consequence lost much of the use of that arm. The joint was in constant danger of separation, thus the requirement to wear a shoulder brace, and he was often in some discomfort. I think this injury would have considerably impeded his ability to climb over the railings as has been suggested. I have noted that the first witness, Mr Stamford, who appears to have been the only person who actually saw my son on the gallery, and whose evidence is therefore of great importance, was quite sure that he did not do so. He describes Frank as standing at the railings and leaning forward to point something out. If by doing so, Frank had perhaps leaned a little further than was wise, and slipped, he would have been less able than most men to save himself from falling.'

The coroner noted this argument but appeared far from convinced. 'There have been statements made about your son's recent despondency, which was thought to be out of character. Can you tell the court about that?'

'I know he was upset by the death of his friend, James Scordell. He died in hospital about a month ago following an operation to reduce a compound fracture of the leg. As to my son's concerns about Mr Geeson, this is the first I have heard of it. He never mentioned it to me. He, Geeson and Scordell were at college together. They were the same age, and members of the same sporting clubs.'

'I assume that his shoulder injury would have put an end to his sporting activities?'

'It did, and of course he regretted it. He had enjoyed both the activity and the camaraderie of the team.'

'Was he in a despondent state because of this?'

'I don't believe so. He had long accepted the situation. He found other activities to occupy him. He made the best of things. He encouraged sports at the school and took satisfaction from the achievements of the pupils. I do not think his injury has any bearing on the matter, other than its role in the accident.'

'Did he have any financial worries? How were his investments performing? Had he received any news of these recently?'

Bradstreet paused as if searching for the right words. 'I regret to say it,' he went on at last, 'but I have seen no evidence of any such investments, and he never mentioned anything of that sort to me. Miss Ellison in her statement has told the court of a conversation in which my son referred to them, and she has also, just today, notified me. I do not disbelieve her, but I have found nothing in his effects to support that statement. I ought to explain that I have examined his papers with great care, in case he had left me a letter, a note, anything which could perhaps throw some light on this dreadful tragedy. There was nothing of that kind, and all his finances were in very good order. He had a modest sum in the bank, but no shares or bonds, or valuable property. Neither did he have any expectations of a legacy.'

'He did not fear that he was in danger of ruin?' asked the coroner. 'Was he in debt?'

'I found no hint of that in his papers. Neither demands from creditors, nor unpaid invoices. He took a small salary from the school, and lived very simply, without extravagance. He has —' here Mr Bradstreet stopped for a while to steady himself 'he had his own rooms at my house, and few expenses.'

'And yet,' said Mr Payne, leaning forward intently, with Miss Ellison's statement grasped firmly between finger and thumb, 'he aspired to have the funds to marry and provide for a family? How did he hope to achieve this?'

Mr Bradstreet made a gesture of helplessness. 'I really cannot say.'

The coroner, with a little grunt of dissatisfaction, decided not to press the witness further.

There was no more testimony to be heard. I felt it most unlikely that the jury would find that the headmaster had been murdered, and their expressions as they held whispered discussions showed that they were hovering uncertainly between the possibility of accident or suicide. They were not required to make that decision, however, since the coroner announced that he would like to receive further information before asking for a verdict and adjourned the hearing for a week.

Inspector Hardiman and Sergeant Lestrade gave nods of acknowledgement in our direction but left together. 'I don't think the jury placed much weight on what I said,' I complained to Holmes after the gentlemen had made their exit.

'No, well, the father is pressing for accidental death and the coroner suspects suicide. You had only just met the man, so your observations on his state of mind will be given less weight than those of the people who knew him. And the coroner was plainly looking for suggestions that your sighting of another person on the gallery might have been mistaken.'

'I know what I saw!' I insisted.

'Yes, and I doubt that a shadow is able to wave a handkerchief to attract attention. You noticed of course that Bradstreet asked the guide, Jarvis, to see if his friend Geeson had returned, and Jarvis went to the library — one passes the library door on the way to the gallery — which means that anyone in the library at that time might have overheard his enquiries and known that Bradstreet was there. If nothing further should emerge, I think the jury will tend towards accident to spare the father's feelings.'

'Do you think Bradstreet was involved in something criminal?' I asked. 'You thought the coded message was between members of a gang.'

'That may still be the case,' said Holmes, 'only not the kind of gang I had envisaged. Consider this — there are three friends, all from the same college, all members of sporting teams: Scordell, recently dead, Bradstreet quite possibly murdered, and Geeson, who has not been seen for a month and could be anywhere. That is unsettling, to say the least.'

'Poor Miss Ellison,' I said. 'Do you think Bradstreet lied to her about his prospects? She would not be the first young lady to be deceived in that way.' I said no more since the subject was indelicate, but in surgery one sometimes saw the dreadful results of the empty promises made by unworthy men.

'I am not so sure,' said Holmes. 'From the little I saw of Bradstreet, he struck me as a well-meaning man who had found himself in a difficult situation. I could be wrong, of course. But I must ask the question, if there really were investments which were so valuable and important to him, why is there no trace of their existence?'

CHAPTER SEVEN

Several days later, I noticed that some of my fellow students were looking at me strangely. One of them even chuckled and nudged me, saying, 'So now we know your secret, Stamford,' which was a little alarming to say the least. There was some comment about a 'pretty young widow' which led me to demand to know what they were talking about. It transpired that an attractive and noticeably distraught young lady in mourning weeds had come to the hospital asking for me by name and had been told to wait for me in the visitors' room. I knew no-one of that description, but protests were useless, and I went to meet her, having gained a wholly unwarranted reputation as a ladies' man.

I was relieved to see that the lady who waited for me was entirely respectable in appearance. She sat alone in a corner, clutching a lace-edged handkerchief. I have seen ladies use such items as little more than a prop to give a semblance of an emotion they do not feel. In this case, the delicate fabric was damp and crushed almost to destruction. The diaphanous dark veil of her bonnet gave the promise of some beauty beneath, and when she lifted that sheer curtain to stare up at me the promise was realised. Her face was a perfect oval, drawn and pale, and the brightest thing about her were her eyes, the margins of which were sore and flushed pink with grief. Her expression of earnest appeal was impossible for any gentleman worthy of that name to resist. I guessed at once who she was, the late Frank Bradstreet's fiancée.

'Mr Stamford?' she asked, in a timid, breathless whisper.

'Yes. And you are Miss Ellison?'

She nodded.

I went to sit by her. 'Is there any way I can assist you?'

She took a moment or two to prepare herself. 'Mr Andrew Bradstreet — my father-in-law as he was to be, told me about the evidence you gave at the inquest on poor Frank. He is certain that there must have been a terrible accident, but he was extremely distressed at the suggestions made in court that it was something far worse. He and I both fear a verdict, a mistaken one, that will leave a stain on Frank's memory which can never be erased.'

I made some expressions of sympathy, which she quietly acknowledged. 'Miss Ellison, before I say any more, I would welcome your opinion on what occurred that day. Not what you hope is true, but what you really think and believe from your own personal knowledge.'

Her eyes took on a dreamy, hopeless look. 'One can never really know someone,' she replied wistfully. 'Frank might have been hiding some failings from me, and from the world. He might have been capable of taking his own life, but I think it would only have been for a noble purpose, to protect others, and not in a selfish or weak way. He was too good a man for that. But Mr Stamford,' she went on, leaning towards me, her tiny fists in their black lace mittens clenching compulsively about the shreds of her handkerchief, 'I need to ask you — I was told that you had said that there was another person with Frank on the whispering gallery just before it happened. And it was no stranger but someone he knew. Did that person not come forward to give evidence?'

'I am afraid not. I hope he recognises his duty and attends when the inquest re-opens, but —'

Miss Ellison said nothing, and I sensed we were thinking the same thing, that there was a sinister reason why that individual had remained silent. There was only one way to proceed.

'I think,' I said, 'you should speak to a friend of mine.'

Fortunately, Holmes was engrossed in his work in the chemistry laboratory, having found fresh inspiration for his experiment. He was more than willing to leave his studies to speak to Miss Ellison. She looked more composed for my brief absence, although when Holmes' tall dark frame loomed in the doorway, with his long almost bone-white face and blazing eyes, she did appear to be a trifle unsettled by the sight. I wondered if there was something about his appearance, his height, perhaps, that reminded her of her lost love.

'Would you like a glass of water, Miss Ellison?' he asked.

She pressed the crumpled handkerchief to her lips. 'Yes, that would be very kind, thank you,' she murmured. Holmes glanced at me wordlessly and I hurried to fetch what was needed. When I returned, they were both sitting silently facing each other. He took the glass and handed it to her. She dabbed an edge of lace to her eyelids and sipped the water.

'Mr Stamford has provided me with a full report of what he saw,' Holmes began. 'I attended the inquest and was particularly interested in the discrepancy between your statement concerning Mr Bradstreet's investments and the evidence of his father. I think that it was the uncertainty regarding his financial situation which prompted the coroner to seek an adjournment in order to acquire further information. Did your fiancé tell you what form his investments took? Did he show you any documents?'

She shook her head sadly. 'No, in fact, when he advised me that he had expectations, I sensed at once that he regretted having told me. Almost immediately he said he was unable to divulge more, and then he asked me not to mention it to anyone, not even his father. He said it would be best for neither of us to refer to it again in future. I had the impression that in some way, revealing what I knew might actually harm his prospects. I have been silent on the subject ever since. I only told his father after — after what happened.'

'But he gave no reason for this secrecy?'

'No. But I can't believe that he was involved in anything that was against the law. He would never have done something of that sort.'

'When, precisely, did he reveal this to you?'

'It was four years ago, when he proposed.'

'Was this before or after you accepted him?'

I saw a brief glow highlight her cheeks. 'I don't know what you are implying, but it was after. I would have accepted him even had he been poor.'

'I am sorry to have offended you,' said Holmes, quickly. 'I am merely trying to gather as much information as I can. And he has never mentioned it again?'

'Not in so many words, no. He often liked to refer to a time when we would be married and said how delightful our lives would be, and I think it was in his mind that we would be very comfortable together. Although —'

'Yes?'

'I feel, I think — he had not done so as much lately. In fact, to be quite truthful, not at all in the last few weeks.' She tormented her handkerchief a little more. 'Although I never talked to him about financial matters, I had the impression that things were not going well for him. I know he was troubled about the cost of repairs needed at the school.'

'The roof was letting in rain?'

'Yes, it was,' she said, surprised at this knowledge. 'I suppose he must have mentioned it. He was always asking the parents for donations to a repair fund, but it was never enough. He worked so very hard.'

'And the injury to his shoulder — how did that affect him? His father said he had overcome his disappointment at not being able to participate in sports. What is your opinion?'

'He was unhappier than he was prepared to say. Those sports which were his favourites, and to which he had devoted so much energy, cricket, rugby football, rowing, were all quite impossible for him. He tried to keep active with walking. He joined a ramblers' club. But it wasn't quite the same. He did think of learning to ride a bicycle, but I told him better not try it in case — in case he fell and hurt himself.' Here she suddenly broke off and her chin quivered, and her eyes moistened. 'I had hoped — I thought — I really thought we would have been married by now. Four years is such a long time to wait, and I could see no end to the waiting. I had begun to think that it might never happen at all. Not from lack of affection, but due to all the many troubles that seemed to afflict him. The things he preferred not to burden me with.'

Neither Holmes nor I were confident about the best way of comforting a weeping maiden. All we could do was adopt sympathetic expressions and wait until she was recovered. After a brief respite, Holmes decided to change the subject.

'Tell me about his college friends, Mr Scordell who I understand died very recently, and Mr Geeson. Have you met them?'

'Yes, I have. Poor Mr Scordell. He was a curator at a gallery of fine art. He was married about a year ago. His wife and I are very friendly. Last month he was injured in a nasty fall in Gresham Street, the place where that warehouse was burned down. The newspapers said it was a very dangerous scene and it was surprising that more were not hurt. He was admitted to this hospital, where he was operated on and left in a terribly weak state. Frank went to visit him. He was very upset to see such a strong man reduced to such incapacity. When Scordell died only a few days later, Frank was deeply affected by it. They had been good friends.'

'What can you tell me about Mr Geeson?'

'I have not met him so often. He appears to be good-natured and gentlemanly, very soft spoken; I would almost say a little bashful. He is not married. I did hear that there is a young lady he admires, but he lacks a fortune and has not been brave enough to address her. He has a curious taste in cravats and handkerchiefs, but I have never heard anything against him.'

Holmes turned to me with a thoughtful expression. 'Stamford, you told me that when Mr Bradstreet looked up at the gallery and saw someone waving a colourful handkerchief, you saw his lips move and you assumed that he was praying.'

'Yes, he seemed to be giving thanks, invoking the name of the Saviour. I don't think he was having a vision.'

'Or could he have been speaking the name of someone he thought he had actually seen? His friend Geeson?'

'Oh, yes, that is possible. I hadn't thought of that. Do you think he might have seen his friend up there?'

'At the very least, he thought he did,' said Holmes. 'He certainly wasn't expecting to see him. Only minutes before he had been told by the guide Jarvis, who had made enquiries in the cathedral library, that Geeson had not returned from the visit to his family.'

'Geeson has been away for some time,' agreed Miss Ellison. 'He didn't come to Scordell's funeral, but the others did.'

There was a moment of quiet. 'The others?' asked Holmes.

CHAPTER EIGHT

Miss Ellison was unaware that she had uttered anything of moment. Seeing our mystification, she went on to enlighten us. 'They were his friends from college. Including Frank there were seven who continued to meet and dine together over the years. For some reason they called themselves the Explorers' Club. It was a silly name, but I didn't dare say so.'

'Why do you call it silly?' I asked, since it sounded rather interesting.

'Because they never went anywhere,' she said contemptuously. 'All they did was talk about it.'

Holmes delivered one of his intense stares, which he probably did not mean to be frightening. 'Tell me about these others,' he said. 'Their names, and what do they do?'

Miss Ellison took a deep gulp from her water glass. 'Well, there is Haxby; his father manages a bank, so after college he went into the bank, where I am sure he does as little as possible. He is one of those men who intends to make his way in life without being useful to anyone but himself. I can't say I care for him. Then there is Tibbott who, so I have been told, is rather too fond of a wager and tries to pretend he is successful, but really I doubt it.' Her tone, if not her words, told us that she didn't care for Tibbott either. 'Argento — his father is an Italian gentleman who collects antiquities, and he acts as his father's English agent. He is always trying to court ladies of fortune, but they always reject him. And Curtis — he is a small man and therefore very loud and thinks everyone should do as he says.'

'Do they meet often?'

'Yes. They dine together regularly at Haxby's club. The Mansion House Club. It is mainly for banking gentlemen.'

I wondered if any of these men had been at the inquest. There had been several of the right age amongst the onlookers, none of whom I had recognised.

'They did not give evidence to the coroner,' said Holmes. 'Of course, they may do so in future.' He remained deep in thought for a while. 'Miss Ellison, if I understand you correctly, your principal concern, in fact your only concern, and the reason you asked to speak to my friend today, is to ascertain the truth behind your fiancé's unfortunate demise?'

'It is.'

'Before I say any more, I feel I should warn you that if you wish to pursue this enquiry, you may find yourself faced with a result which will be worse than not knowing,' said Holmes, gently. 'You must prepare yourself to learn a painful truth.'

Miss Ellison, who had appeared to me at first like a black ribbon drooping inconsolably from a mourning wreath, now sat up straight with resolve. 'I am prepared,' she said. 'But what can I do? Whom may I trust? If Mr Scordell was alive and Mr Geeson here, I might have gone to either of them for advice, but the others I am far less sure of.'

Holmes rose to his feet and paced back and forth as he often did when determining on a course of action. Miss Ellison followed his movements with her eyes as if she was observing a wild creature in its native habitat, uncertain of which way it would jump. He turned to face her. 'I do have something of a reputation for solving mysteries,' he said, 'but I have no official status and cannot therefore demand that people tell me what I need to know. You, on the other hand, Miss Ellison, are able to request information with far greater prospect of success.'

'You may have complete trust in Holmes,' I said, encouragingly. 'Not only his ability to untangle the most complex of mysteries, which I have seen him do before, but also his absolute secrecy and delicacy.'

She said nothing in reply, but a whole volume of expressions passed across her features. She dried her eyes, opened her reticule, and drew out an envelope. 'I have received a letter,' she said. 'It is from Frank.' She extended a trembling hand and held the missive out to Holmes, who took it and removed the folded paper from the envelope.

'This is his handwriting?' he said.

'Yes, I am very familiar with it.'

'I have your permission to read it aloud?'

'Yes, please do.'

He nodded. 'The letter is dated July 1872. *My dearest Margaret, By accepting my proposal of marriage, you have made me the happiest of men. I long for the day when we will be united.*' Holmes gave a little cough, by which I gathered he was somewhat embarrassed by the tender nature of the words, although in his flat dry tones there was no hint of the emotions being communicated. '*I mentioned in the warmth of that dear moment that I have expectations of wealth, and in doing so, I revealed a secret which is known only to a few. That wealth I intend to be the foundation of our future lives together. If it should come to pass that some disaster should prevent our marriage, it is my wish that you will be the sole beneficiary of my investment when it matures.*

'*I have entrusted this letter to a legal man, who does not know its contents. His only instruction is to send it to you if the worst should happen. If you receive this, I wish you to go to James Scordell or Edmund Geeson, good friends of mine, either of whom will be able to advise you further, both of whom you can trust to carry out my wishes.*

'Hmm,' said Holmes. 'The letter ends with assurances of eternal love.' He studied the paper. 'It is written on the headed notepaper of the school in black ink with a J nib. There is no doubt in my mind that this is the work of Frank Bradstreet. Miss Ellison, do you know if your fiancé left a will?'

'Nothing has been found in his papers,' she said. 'No solicitor has brought anything to his father's notice.'

'If there is no will, then how will his estate be distributed?'

'He has — had — no brothers or sisters, and his mother died many years ago. I would imagine that his father is his only close relative and will receive everything. I had assumed, from what Frank told me, that he had been putting aside funds into his investment and that it would now be a useful sum, but his father has told me that the estate, which is mainly Frank's personal effects and a small figure in the bank, amounts to a very small value.'

'The school?'

'That is in the hands of trustees.'

'And will form no part of his estate. So, his fortune, if there is one, is mainly composed of this mysterious investment which he means you to have. Something which is not supported by any official document and is not mentioned in a will. Something which he clearly did not want his father or anyone outside his closest friends to know about.'

'It seems so.'

'I don't suppose there are any papers amongst his effects which appear to be simply a list of numbers? He might have recorded these secret investments in such a manner, something known only to himself?'

'I don't know that there was anything of that nature. Mr Bradstreet has not mentioned it. Mr Holmes, what should I do?'

'I suggest, to begin with, that you call on Mr Scordell's widow, and see what you can learn. If she has a story to tell, bring her to me. You may urge upon her the importance of preserving your fiancé's reputation. Do not show her the letter. In fact, show it to no-one and do not mention the contents to anyone. I appreciate that your statement to the coroner's court did refer to the investment, but in the absence of any evidence that it exists, I feel that despite the fact you did not know of it until after you had accepted him, the world will dismiss it as an empty promise made to secure your hand. This unflattering assumption may pain you, but I urge you to leave it at that for the present.' He returned the letter. 'Mr Geeson — do you know his family?'

'I am afraid I do not. I don't have his address.'

Holmes presented his card. 'Perhaps Mrs Scordell will know. Let me know what you discover. Oh, and one other thing would assist me. Did your fiancé retain the college yearbooks relating to the time he and his friends were there?'

'I'm not sure.'

'If not, perhaps Mrs Scordell might have them amongst her husband's effects. I would like to examine them.'

'I'll see what I can find.' The first hint of a smile graced her features. 'I — I don't know what to say, Mr Holmes. You have been so very helpful and yet we have only just made each other's acquaintance.'

'Think nothing of it,' he said, with an airy wave of the hand. 'I devote my life to the solution of mysteries, the cultivation of the intellect. It will be my pleasure.'

Miss Ellison bid us good-day and took her leave with rather more energy in her demeanour than she had demonstrated earlier.

'Poor lady,' I said, 'I do hope we might help her. She is obviously quite distraught by her loss.'

'Yes, that was a fine display with the handkerchief,' said Holmes, dismissively. 'But I sense anger, as well as grief. After four years of friendship and four of betrothal, I can well imagine that Miss Ellison, whose age I estimate at nearer thirty than twenty-five, is seeing the lost years stretching behind her and the looming spectre of spinsterhood. Her description of Mr Bradstreet's college friends demonstrated that none of them have earned her admiration or look to be material she would consider fit for a husband.'

'It is a little soon for her to be thinking about that!' I exclaimed.

'Do not underestimate the capriciousness of womankind,' said Holmes.

I thought that statement was a little cruel on his part but did not say so. 'So, the message in secret code was between a headmaster and a librarian who were college friends,' I said. 'Not quite the desperate criminals you had in mind.'

'And yet men are dead,' he said. 'Two that we know of, and there may be more. This is not some trivial game. There is much at stake, and real danger to those who might uncover the mystery. That is why I told Miss Ellison not to make any further mention of the investment.'

I felt a chill of fear slither lizard-like up my spine. 'Are we in danger?' I asked.

'Perhaps. We already know too much.'

Once again, I had been unwittingly plunged into a frightening situation due to my friendship with Holmes, and once again, I would not have sought to change that for anything.

CHAPTER NINE

Two days later, following an exchange of messages, it was agreed that Miss Ellison would accompany Mrs Scordell to partake of tea and be interviewed by Holmes. My friend was a little surprised when I observed that I did not think his room, with its pervading aroma of pipe smoke, piles of disorganised papers and saucers overflowing with dottle, would be the best place to entertain ladies; however, he reluctantly took my point. It was futile to ask him to change his arrangements, so I therefore prepared my own humble accommodation for the visitors. My lodgings, which consisted of two rooms above a small bootmaker's shop in Farringdon, were modest yet respectable, not so close to the Metropolitan Railway to be disturbed by the noise of passing trains, and conveniently, mere minutes' walk from the hospital. A clean cloth on the table, a posy of dried flowers, and a tray of tea things were all that was needed. My mother had been generous with a donation of little pastries, and it all looked rather dainty and genteel.

As we waited for our guests to arrive, Holmes fitted his long frame into an easy chair and studied the coded message once more. 'Four dead, suspect murder, danger to you three. Taken together, the dead, the endangered, one or more suspects, and the writer, Mr Bradstreet, makes at least nine persons. Had he not died that day, he would have told me all, or at least I would have learned it.'

'Do you have any theories?' I asked.

'It is a grievous error to form theories on insufficient information,' Holmes said. 'Oh, one should be free to examine all the possibilities, but a theory can be a dangerous thing. Men find it too easy to attach themselves to an idea of their own creation and are then unwilling or unable to abandon it, even in the face of compelling new facts. All I know at present is that Bradstreet and six others were once college friends and members of sporting clubs, who still meet and dine together. I am aware that certain things can be taken very seriously, but I have never yet heard of a murderous disagreement in team sports. Well — not at either of our oldest universities.'

'What about their studies? Their professional interests?' I ventured. 'There may be rivalries to discover.'

'Perhaps,' mused Holmes, sounding unconvinced as he so often did when I offered my suggestions. 'If I can view the college yearbooks, they might provide something of interest, a starting point for further enquiries. The problem which impedes my progress is that there is a situation underlying these tragedies which is being kept a close secret, the subject of coded messages between friends, and those who know the secret dare not speak of it.'

'I assume that the fact that the message was to be delivered by Bradstreet's servant meant that Mr Geeson, had he received it, would have known who it came from,' I said. 'Otherwise, there is no signature, and nothing in the message to identify the writer.'

Holmes suddenly sat up straight and turned to me with a very shocked expression.

'Holmes? Whatever is the matter?' I asked.

'The matter, Stamford,' he exclaimed with some energy, 'is that I am a blind imbecile and cannot see a vital clue when it stares me in the face.' He was about to explain this outburst when the landlady knocked at my door and announced that two ladies had come to take tea.

When our visitors were admitted, I was extremely glad that I had determined that the meeting would not take place in Holmes' rooms. Mrs Scordell, who was scarcely older than me, was in that interesting state of health which would normally have been the crown to a happy marriage. As it was, the young widow looked wholly defeated by her position and could not have anticipated the coming family event with any pleasure. Miss Ellison, who I think was anxious to have something useful to do, made a great fuss over her companion, whom she had assisted up the stairs. Once in my little parlour, she took great pains to ensure that the widow was comfortable and well supplied with tea and urged her to eat something to keep up her strength. It was some minutes before we could proceed. Once we were all settled, Mrs Scordell, who was carrying a small package wrapped in paper, passed it to Holmes. He unwrapped it and smiled to see a collection of college yearbooks.

'I am so grateful to have a sympathetic ear,' said Mrs Scordell at last, staring disconsolately into her teacup, the contents of which offered no enlightenment. 'I have always felt there was something about my poor husband's death that should have been investigated. I have told so many people of this, but you are the first to have listened. He detested noise and crowds and smells, so I cannot imagine why he was in Gresham Street anywhere near the scene of that terrible fire. According to the newspapers it went on for days, and it was a horrid sight — people choking on the smoke and fumes, and all around were thieves and vagabonds and fights, and the police had to be called to restore order and disperse everyone. No decent person would have gone there.'

'He had no business which might have taken him there?' asked Holmes.

'None that I know of.'

'His friend Mr Bradstreet; his school is on Noble Street, which is very near. Might he have gone to visit?'

'I don't believe he ever went to the school. Mr Bradstreet often came to dine with us.'

Holmes nodded and sat back in a contemplative manner. 'Tell me about your husband's profession.'

'He was at Capital Fine Art in Brook Street,' said Mrs Scordell, waving away an offering of another pastry from Miss Ellison. 'They sell oil paintings and watercolours and sculptures. It is a highly respectable business. He loved his work.'

'Miss Ellison has told me that Mr Bradstreet had some troubles on his mind in the last few weeks. Do you know if he discussed his concerns with your husband?'

'I know that they talked a great deal during that time. I mean, more than usual. It was after Mr Bradstreet went away for a few days — when he came back, he and my husband and their friend Mr Geeson all met up and talked. But I don't know what they talked about.'

'Where did they meet?'

'At a coffee house near Brook Street, if it was all three. Sometimes they met up with Geeson at St Paul's.'

Holmes turned to Miss Ellison. 'When did Mr Bradstreet go away?'

'It was in the middle of September,' she said.

'And for what purpose?'

'It was a rest cure. At least that was the intention. Frank had been working hard preparing for the next school year. As you know, he was worried about the cost of repairs needed to the school and had been trying to find ways of raising funds. He wrote to all the parents and was trying to organise a bazaar. He told me that he felt a little jaded and his doctor had suggested he spend some time away from London, in the country or by the sea, to get some sunshine and fresh air, which would restore his health. I wanted to accompany him, but he said it would be better if I did not because of — appearances. He was very thoughtful that way. He didn't want people to talk.'

'Do you know where he went? How long was he away? Did you have any letters from him?'

'He did mention Dorset. But there were no letters, and he never told me exactly where he was going. He thought he might be gone for at least a week, perhaps two or more, and he promised to write, so I was very surprised when he came back only three or four days later. I could tell that it had not gone well. He was pale, almost shockingly so. He did not look as if he had been outdoors in the air at all. When I asked if he was unwell, he only said that the diet had disagreed with him. I accepted that explanation at the time, but now — I don't know — I can't help thinking that perhaps he was hiding something from me.'

'His father never mentioned this visit or the reason for it at the inquest,' I said.

'Perhaps he felt it might influence the jury's verdict in an unwanted direction,' said Holmes.

Miss Ellison said nothing, but her eyes spoke for her.

'And it was soon after his return when he had this meeting with Mr Geeson and Mr Scordell?'

'Yes, it was the very next day.'

Holmes turned back to Mrs Scordell. 'I have always believed that a world of pain and confusion could be avoided if husbands confided their deepest fears to their wives,' he said. 'Is there anything you can say to enlighten us?'

'The only worry which James shared with me concerned his work at Brook Street. I don't think there was any connection to his friends.'

'Nevertheless, it would be interesting to know more,' said Holmes, persuasively. He did have an unusually soft tone of voice with which he was able to induce timid persons to tell him what he wanted to know, and sometimes more than they had intended to reveal. It was especially effective with females, and Mrs Scordell was no exception.

'It was a few months ago. Capital Fine Art was mounting a special exhibition of sacred art, and there was one item which attracted a great deal of interest. Several of the pieces in the exhibition, including this one, were sold to collectors, but shortly after the sale, doubts were raised as to its authenticity. That is really all I know, except that the business was, for a time, in danger of being sued. The notoriety would have greatly harmed its standing. James had not been personally involved, so I think his concern was more for the reputation of his employers than his own position.'

'Did he talk to Mr Bradstreet about this?'

'I think he talked about business matters to all his friends. They are educated men, men of the world. They all reassured him that if it was ever required, they would be honoured to vouch for his good character. Mr Haxby said that as long as his bank account was spotless, no-one could accuse him of anything. Mr Argento, who knows a great many people who are well-known collectors of art, said that, if necessary, he would introduce him to an experienced man who could advise him.'

'Who was this man?'

'I don't know. I don't think the meeting ever took place. James did consult a knowledgeable gentleman, a Mr

Vambrook, who is a collector of many things, books and pictures and old writings. I think they became acquainted because Mr Vambrook often visited Brook Street. But in the end, the matter was privately resolved between the business and the buyer in an amicable manner. And the owners exonerated James from all fault.'

I arranged for fresh tea to be brought, and while we waited Holmes was thoughtfully leafing through the yearbooks, when he paused and gave a smile of satisfaction.

'I see that your husband was a member of a rowing team at college?'

'Yes, he was.'

'A coxed eight, I see.'

'Yes, I believe so.'

He tapped a page with a long finger. 'The participants listed here in order are Bullstrode, Haxby, Bradstreet, Scordell, Argento, Tibbott, Geeson, Rellish, and Curtis.'

'Yes, those names sound familiar.'

'And seven of the team members were in the habit of dining regularly at Haxby's club, the Mansion House?'

'Yes, all except Bullstrode and Rellish.'

'What can you tell me about them?'

'Bullstrode was one of my husband's closest friends at college. After he completed his studies, his father sent him out to Darjeeling to manage some properties. We have the occasional letter from there. I suppose,' she sighed, 'I ought to write to him. Really, it has been so hard to know what to do. Rellish, I don't know. I don't believe I ever met him.'

Holmes questioned Mrs Scordell about the other members of the Explorers' Club, but she had no more information than Miss Ellison. By the time this was done, it was clear that she was tiring. We drank more tea and finished the pastries, then I went to hire a hansom to take our visitors home.

'What have you discovered?' I asked Holmes after the ladies had left. I was relieved to see them safely on their way. Pleasant as their company had been, Mrs Scordell's advanced condition and her emotional fragility had made me concerned that I might have to assist at an event for which my study of ophthalmology had left me wholly unprepared.

'It was your comment concerning the sender of the message that alerted me,' said Holmes. 'The absence of a signature. What if the word "three" at the close of the message was the signature? In the team of rowers, we have Bradstreet, the sender of the message, listed as number three. Scordell, the recently deceased, is number four. The numbers in the coded message did not therefore refer to numbers of persons, but to individuals, who are designated by their position as oarsmen. That is a good way of including them in the message without resorting to putting their names into the code.'

'And Bullstrode and Rellish?' I asked.

'Yes, they are the only two members of the rowing team not included in the seven who meet to dine. And quite possibly they are the only two who might be persuaded to reveal what they know. Bullstrode, who may still be in Darjeeling, is less likely to be a source of useful information, which leaves me to try and locate Mr Rellish.'

CHAPTER TEN

The resumed sitting of the inquest on Frank Bradstreet had been covered by all the leading newspapers. It was the subject of an especially detailed report in *The Times*, which did not think of itself as a sensational publication but could cheerfully venture into that field if it chose. This naturally led to an extended and largely ill-informed and speculative correspondence in the pages of that newspaper.

The only letter I thought to be of any interest was from a doctor. Claiming a long experience of disorders of the brain, he reported that it sometimes occurred that a gentleman became convinced, on the flimsiest of evidence, that he would suddenly acquire great wealth, but on examination of the facts this was often found to be a delusion. Some men he had known had been able to maintain that delusion throughout their lives and died with it intact. He thought that such men were often the happier for it, although the obsession tended to distress their families. In other cases, where the light of reason had dawned and shown the belief for what it was worth, the result was often a broken mind. These unhappy souls had to be carefully watched, as the blow to their expectations could lead to self-destruction. This letter had provoked an immediate response from Mr Bradstreet senior. He objected to the inference of suicide in the strongest possible terms and pointed out that the medical man had never so much as met his son and could not therefore express an opinion on his state of mind.

Although the death of Scordell appeared to be no more than an unfortunate accident, Holmes decided to make some enquiries and it was the ever-helpful Nurse Harmon who showed us the record of the patient's admission to the hospital. The truth was far worse than I had imagined. Early one morning, a carrier passing down Gresham Street had heard some groans coming from the still slightly smoking ruins of the burned-out furniture warehouse. When he'd gone to investigate, he'd discovered a terribly injured man who'd appeared to have fallen into a basement after the collapse of some weakened flooring. It had taken the combined efforts of the police, the fire brigade and the labourers who had been working on the demolition to recover the man without danger to themselves and to convey him to Barts. He had not been in the basement the previous afternoon and it was thought that he might have missed his way in the dark; either that or he had quite deliberately gone to look at the site out of curiosity and the weakened floor had collapsed under his feet.

On examination, he was found to have suffered numerous injuries. There was a multiple compound fracture of the lower bones of one leg, fragments of which were protruding through the skin, and both his ankles were dislocated, showing that he had been standing when he dropped through the floor and landed on his feet. He had also suffered abrasions to his face and hands, some scorching from the residual heat and damage to his lungs from inhaling the poisonous fumes of burned varnish. The pain of his injuries was so great that he was barely coherent, and it was decided to apply chloroform when restoring the leg fracture. This exercise had taken some considerable time to achieve. He was eventually made as comfortable as possible, with his leg supported by splints and bandages, and soothing lotions were applied to his burns.

'He was in such a terrible way that we only admitted family to see him and those friends to whom he was especially close,' said Nurse Harmon. 'But the visits had to be kept very brief and limited to one person at a time, as they were distressing to everyone concerned. His poor wife, who was in a delicate condition, took one look at him and fainted away.'

'Did he provide any clues as to how the accident had come about?' asked Holmes. 'I have spoken to the widow, who could think of no reason why he would have been in Gresham Street, and she thought him too careful a man to take such a foolish risk.'

'He was hardly able to speak, although he was desperate to do so. I heard him say something about some papers he had lost, and meeting a gentleman. That was all.'

'Were any papers found nearby? Was that what he was concerned about? Men in *extremis* often revert to expressing their last wishes.'

'There was nothing of any special moment. The contents of his pockets, the usual items men carry, a pocketbook, money, tobacco and so on, were given to his widow after his death. There were no documents. There was some burnt paper in the basement, but it was thought it must have been part of a record book belonging to the warehouse. The pages were too damaged to be read.'

'Tell me about his death.'

'He seemed to be making a slow recovery — in fact, at first we had good hopes of him because he was young and strong, although we could not say if he would walk again. But then he went into a decline, and a few days later he died. There was a post-mortem examination, which concluded that the ultimate cause of death was exhaustion and the effects of chloroform on a fatty liver. The inquest was held here, and the verdict was that he had died from complications of injuries suffered in an accident. Everything was done to save him.'

'Fatty liver always seems to be found where there is a death under chloroform,' I said. 'Unfortunately, one can never detect its existence until the man is dead.'

'It would be most useful if we could detect it before the chloroform is applied,' said Holmes. 'Of course, if we were to discover that all men have some small degree of fatty liver, we would have to look elsewhere for cause of death, which would be very inconvenient.'

I detected a satirical note in his voice. Surgeons, understandably, do not like to have their competence called into question, and some can be eager to grasp at an easy explanation for the death of a patient. Before I was a student, I worked at Barts as a surgical dresser and often assisted John Watson, whose dedication and nerve are second to none. I have observed the application of chloroform many times, and it is a wonderful but dangerous chemical about which we still know far too little. A heavy fluid, it is highly destructive of animal flesh, and on evaporation, which it does readily, it releases a pungent and potentially lethal vapour. When that vapour is mixed with a large volume of air, however, it performs miracles of alleviating pain. Too much, too long, too strong, will harm the patient and it is a delicate balance of which every surgeon must be aware. Deaths from chloroform do occur from time to time and can be rapid and unpredictable. I hoped that science would one day find a solution.

'And now we have further mysteries,' said Holmes, when Nurse Harmon had gone to replace the patient ledger. 'Scordell spoke of meeting a gentleman. A gentleman who lured him into danger, perhaps? And what of the damaged papers, which are long gone, now? They might mean nothing or everything. But I have to ask, if the papers in the basement were Scordell's, and he had dropped them in there and fallen when he tried to retrieve them, was the heat which remained from the fire sufficient to burn them beyond recognition?'

I saw where his thoughts were leading. 'You think Scordell may also have been murdered?'

'I would not rule it out. There are dark secrets, in this case, Stamford. I see them, just a hint of them in every place I look. My task is to expose them to the light.'

I determined, on returning to my studies, to set aside some time to seek more information on the facts of Scordell's death by applying myself diligently to the writings of Her Majesty's own personal anaesthetist, the late lamented John Snow, on the action of chloroform. In the event I learned nothing to assist me regarding the death of Scordell, but I did learn much for which I would later be extremely grateful.

CHAPTER ELEVEN

When the inquest on Frank Bradstreet resumed, the coroner, while taking care not to mention the contents of the letters recently published in the press, stated only that the jurymen, if they had read mentions of the case in the newspapers either in reports or correspondence, should pay no attention to them, but address themselves only to the evidence placed before the court.

'It is a hard task to put something like that out of one's mind,' I said to Holmes.

'Impossible,' said Holmes. 'There are whole professions both legal and otherwise whose entire operation depends upon that being the case.'

The first witness to be called was a rather unusual-looking man, a little over medium height but almost as broad, wearing round spectacles. His dark hair was combed very flat, his face pale and fleshy. 'My name is Ruben Argento,' he said. 'I am Italian by birth. I am thirty-two years of age, and I devote myself to the collection of works of Italian art. I have known Frank Bradstreet for many years. We were at college together.'

Mr Argento, I recalled, had once been a member of the college rowing team, presumably when he presented a less substantial version of his current figure. His hands were large and soft-looking and there was a heavy gold ring on one finger. His whole demeanour was that of a quietly successful man whose athletic pretensions lay in his youthful past and who had since devoted his leisure hours to enjoying the finer pleasures of the table and wine cellar.

'Can you tell the court if Mr Bradstreet ever purchased works of art or expressed an interest in doing so?' asked the coroner.

'No, he did neither as far as I am aware. I had the impression that his purse would not be sufficient for that. I declined to embarrass him by making the suggestion.'

'Did he ever discuss investments with you? Do you know if he had any money or valuables put aside for the future?'

'I do not think he had possessions of that nature. But he did not discuss his personal finances with me.'

'Can you tell the court anything out of the ordinary you might have observed recently about his state of mind? Had there been any change in him?'

Mr Argento spent some moments considering this question. 'All I can say,' he said at last, 'is that in the last few weeks he had been very quiet, less communicative than before. I did ask him what the matter was as I thought he might be unwell, and he brushed the question aside. Had he been in need of money I would have gladly lent him some, and he knew it. He had only to ask. When I thought more of it, I suspected that he was brooding about the death of his friend Scordell, who passed away recently following an accident. They were almost like brothers, and he was to be godfather to Scordell's firstborn.'

'Do you have any theories as to why he fell from the gallery of St Paul's?'

Mr Argento paused again. He removed his spectacles and polished them with a snowy white handkerchief, then replaced them. 'I have no theories,' he said at last. 'He was my friend, and I suppose I prefer to think that it was an accident, brought about by the weakness in his shoulder, which was wont to collapse if he was not careful. Maybe he gripped the railings and his shoulder joint suddenly separated and he lost his balance.' He gave a helpless shrug. 'That is all I can think of.'

Argento was allowed to sit down, and the next person to be called was Alban Haxby. He was as far distant in appearance from his predecessor as it was possible to be, a slim, well-set-up man, with a brush of auburn hair, strong handsome features, and a confident manner. It was a banker's confidence. It came from having money, of having always had money and the certainty that he would never be without money. I could easily imagine him as a rower or cricketer or pounding down a muddy field clutching a rugby ball, and handing off challenges with a stiff arm and a look of contempt.

'Mr Haxby, you have heard what Mr Argento has said, and I would like you to tell the court if you had any knowledge regarding Mr Bradstreet's finances or his state of mind.'

'All I know about his finances was that he never seemed to have any,' said Haxby with a little laugh that seemed out of place on such an occasion. 'He was always trying to make a penny do the work of a shilling, if you see what I mean. Donations to the school building fund were very welcome. It was a hand-to-mouth business, and was not, I think, in a position to meet a large expense. When he said the roof needed a repair, which he could ill afford, I said he ought to ask the bank for a loan, but he wouldn't consider it, as he had an aversion to debt. Debts always have to be repaid, and I don't think he could see his way of ever being free of them.' He shook his head as if this was a sad reflection on his late friend's acumen.

'You are saying that he was anxious about money?'

'Yes. Constantly.'

'Would you agree with Mr Argento that the death of his friend Scordell had been a hard blow to him?'

'He didn't talk about it — I suppose so. But a man doesn't make away with himself over such a thing, does he?' He gave another laugh. 'I mean, I can't imagine that.'

The coroner had no further questions of Haxby.

The next witness was Tibbott. I could see why Miss Ellison disliked him. Although outwardly respectable in his attire, and well-groomed as to hair and beard, he had a watchful manner, his eyes darting here and there. His hands and fingers were strong and deft, and he moved them constantly, like a musician practising an invisible instrument. In an older man I might have suspected palsy, but in Tibbott it appeared more as a habit he could not break.

Curtis was the last to be called. From his diminutive stature and slight build, I guessed he was the coxswain of the rowing crew. He had a curious posture, shoulders tensed back, chin a little raised, arms folded in front, and spoke as if making an announcement to a crowded arena. Had he been clean shaven, he might have been mistaken for a schoolboy, and to avoid that embarrassment and leave his majority in no doubt, he had grown a set of light brown whiskers which framed his face like an Elizabethan ruff.

Neither of these witnesses could add anything to the story. Both, when pressed, said they thought their friend's death had been an accident.

Mr Payne took a few moments to neaten his pile of papers and addressed the court. 'It was my intention to conclude the inquest today,' he said, 'but I have unexpectedly received a letter from a gentleman who has some new information to place before the court which may be relevant to the proceedings. He is willing to travel from Scotland to give evidence, and I have asked him to do so. I will therefore adjourn once more, in order that we might hear him.'

The members of the Explorers' Club were clearly disturbed by this unforeseen announcement. There were whispers and gestures, and Haxby even rose to his feet to demand something of the coroner, with Argento pulling at his arm in an effort to dissuade him.

'That is all, gentlemen,' said Payne, very firmly, and he rose and left the room. The jury filed out, their faces stern in dissatisfaction at the further duties required of them. As the members of the Explorers' Club made their departures, I saw Holmes give each of them one of his searching looks.

Holmes and I were preparing to leave when a youthful, rather anxious-looking man approached me. 'Mr Stamford? I recall you gave evidence at the first hearing. I hope you don't mind my addressing you; my name is Nevins, and I am with the library at St Paul's. I was hoping to be called as a witness today, but it seems the coroner did not think it necessary.'

'But you believe you have some relevant information?' asked Holmes, suddenly towering over us both, his long nose prodding inquisitively. Mr Nevins jumped like a startled rabbit at the abrupt intrusion. 'I accompanied Mr Stamford on his visit to the late Mr Bradstreet,' Holmes explained, 'and I find the whole affair very curious. I am anxious to know more.'

'It may or may not be of importance,' said Nevins, 'but it struck me that if Mr Bradstreet saw someone waving a colourful handkerchief, a yellow one, as you said, that means he must have thought he saw his friend Mr Geeson, who often displayed such an item. Geeson was otherwise very quiet and simple in his attire, and it was his habit that if he wanted to attract the notice of a friend when in a crowd or some way distant, rather than calling out, he used to wave the handkerchief.'

'But as we know, Mr Geeson has not been at the library for some time,' I said. 'Bradstreet could not have seen him.'

'That is true. Bradstreet must have been mistaken. No-one has seen Geeson there recently. The thing is — Geeson is a friend of mine and I am very worried about him. Oh, I know he has written more than once to say he is in Lincolnshire on family business, but I am not at all sure that he is.'

CHAPTER TWELVE

Nevins, having made that disconcerting statement, looked at us both appealingly.

'Excuse me,' said Holmes, 'but are you quite certain that the letters from Geeson were actually from him?'

'Oh yes, or at least, we have never questioned it. In the library we are very familiar with his writing and manner of address, and really, I don't think they could have come from anyone else. But since you mention it, his penmanship was unusually shaky, and I did wonder if he was indisposed or unsettled in some way.'

'Is that the only reason for your concern?' I asked. 'He might have written the letters in a great hurry.'

'No, it is not. The fact is, I have been worried about him for some little while. Geeson is usually a cheerful, good-tempered fellow. But not long before he went away, his manner changed. When I asked him what the matter was, he said only that he thought he had been badly betrayed by an old friend. I asked him for more details, but he said he could tell me no more. He never mentioned his family at all. He went about his normal pursuits and engagements, working at the library, paying visits to acquaintances. Then, quite suddenly, he was gone.'

'What makes you so sure that he is not with his family, perhaps dealing with an unexpected illness or a bereavement?' Holmes asked. 'That would easily explain his hurried penmanship.'

Nevins looked about him as if worried he might be overheard, but there was no-one in earshot. 'He is not with his family. I am sure of it,' he said. He seemed unwilling to say more.

'Mr Bradstreet's fiancée Miss Ellison has asked me to assist her in clarifying the circumstances of his death,' said Holmes. 'It might cast some light on the mystery if I was to learn what was troubling Mr Geeson, something that he might have confided in his friend. I would very much like to speak with him. I am willing to try and help you to discover his whereabouts, but I need to know all that you can tell me.'

Nevins hesitated, then nodded. 'There is a matter concerning his family of which only his closest friends are aware. I will reveal what I know because of how worried I am, but please, I beg of you, promise me that you will not reveal this to another soul. He would be most upset to have it generally known.'

'I promise,' said Holmes, and I echoed the assurance.

'Geeson's mother died about five years ago,' began Nevins. 'Soon afterwards, in fact, suspiciously soon, his father brought another woman into the house. She was not a good type of woman. I will say no more than that of her. Geeson understandably felt that this was a gross insult to his mother's memory, and he revealed this opinion to his father. He is a quiet man, but he has deep feelings, and on this occasion, he did not fear to express them. There was a dreadful quarrel, in which Geeson made no attempt to conceal his low opinion of his father's choice, and they parted on bad terms. Some while later Geeson returned to Lincolnshire, hoping to heal the breach, but his father, abetted by his new companion, wouldn't allow him in the house. I don't know what words were said during that visit, but they must have been terrible indeed. Geeson told me he could never go back there. Since then, he has heard from a friend that his father has now married this woman and she stands to inherit all his property. So Geeson has lost all his expectations. He has never spoken of it again.'

'What is the address in Lincolnshire?' asked Holmes.

'Stoneleigh; it is an estate, near South Brantby.'

'He might be there if there has been a change of heart. Have you written to him?'

'Yes, but I received no reply. I did fear that some accident had befallen him, but I have heard no news from that part of the world, and I began to wonder if he had ever gone there at all. Then my letter was returned to me unopened. After a week or two I went to his lodgings to enquire after him. The landlady told me that Geeson had gone away but he had not told her where he was going. He paid her a month's rent in advance, but she has heard nothing from him since.'

'When and where did you last see him? Please be as precise as you can.'

'I last saw him in the library at St Paul's. I don't recall the exact date, but it was not long after he had told me about his friend Scordell's accident. Scordell suffered a bad fall at the place where that fire was, in Gresham Street. Geeson went to see him in hospital, but his friend was so drugged with soporifics he hardly knew anyone was there. Geeson was very upset. The man died about a week later.'

'Can you describe Mr Geeson to me? You say he dresses very plainly. Is there anything about him which is distinctive apart from his unusual handkerchief?'

'Well, he is a tall man, almost as tall as you, although because of his natural timidity he tries to conceal it. He's very slender, wears his hair over-long, and he has pince-nez for reading.'

'Were you at St Paul's on the day of Bradstreet's death?'

'Yes, I was. I was in the library. Of course, I didn't see what happened. No-one there did. We didn't know anything about it until we heard the screams and the crash and rushed out to look.'

'But you would have been there when the guide, Jarvis, came in to ask if Geeson had returned?'

'Yes, I was.'

'Did he mention Bradstreet by name?'

Nevins considered this. 'I am not sure, he might have done, or at least he said that it was Geeson's friend, the same friend who had been there asking about him before.'

'After Jarvis departed, but before Bradstreet's death, did you notice if anyone left the library?'

'I — don't think so. There were several scholars at work, and of course the librarians on duty that day.' Nevins frowned in thought. 'I recall when we heard the commotion, the scholars did not leave their seats at once — they are often quite deaf to the world when they are deep in their manuscripts — but some of the staff went to see what had occurred. All the staff were there at the time, apart from Geeson. When they came back, they were very shocked and upset, and said no-one was to go out until told to do so. Then the police came and questioned us all. No-one could tell them anything.'

'You don't recall any of the scholars leaving the library shortly before Bradstreet fell?'

'No, but it is possible, of course. Oh, I see what you mean, such a man could be a valuable witness. But if he is, he has not come forward.'

Holmes thanked Nevins, asking to be contacted if any other thoughts came to mind, or if he received any new information, and cards were exchanged.

'Betrayal,' said Holmes thoughtfully, as we departed to return to our studies. 'I wonder what kind of betrayal Geeson suspected and who his suspect was.'

'What do you make of the Explorers' Club members?' I asked. 'I know your powers of observation will have enlightened you more than I was.'

He smiled at the compliment. 'Men and women often have small signs about their persons that can reveal a great deal, if one knows what to look for. They often indicate a trade or profession, or even a history, without being aware of it. Haxby, however, is an empty suit of fine clothes, that indicate no great activity. He is a shell of a man with nothing inside.

'As to Tibbott, I would not care to play cards with him, at least not for money. He has that way of moving his fingers as if to constantly exercise them, which I have seen in only two professions: magicians and card sharps. Did you notice the cut of his cuffs? Ah, no, I see you did not. Miss Ellison said that Tibbott wants us to think he is a successful gambler on his own talents, but those are rare creatures indeed. He might be a cheat who has not yet been found out, or he makes nothing out of it and is bankrolled from another source.

'The cuffs and fingers of Mr Curtis reveal that he uses a pen in his work, but not so shiny or deeply inked as to suggest clerking, which would be unlikely for a college man. His manner and general carriage suggest a wish to command, and I would assume therefore he has a minor role in government service. If he had already achieved a position of note he would make a point of mentioning it, but he does not. Doing so would only draw attention to his humble status of which his friends would be aware.

'Contrast him with Argento, who is a shrewd man and prefers us to underestimate him. But he is weighed down by good living and ought to lose some flesh so that the knee that begins to trouble him can heal.

'I will make some enquiries — I have sources, a family connection who might be able to tell me a little more. Even the smallest fragment of information could be vital. There are dark clouds hiding a deadly truth, and with diligence I will sweep them away.'

CHAPTER THIRTEEN

In Holmes' absence I was able to devote some uninterrupted time to my studies, but I also set aside an afternoon to pay a visit to the British Museum, where my friend George Luckhurst had recently been appointed as assistant keeper of Greek and Roman antiquities. He had been working on a new exhibition, and I was entertained with a special tour. The salary from this junior post was augmented by an annuity from his late aunt and this had enabled him to take some pleasant rooms not far from the museum, which he had proceeded to furnish according to his taste. Naturally he was as yet unable to acquire the genuine works of art he would have liked, but the pictures and ornaments he had chosen were highly decorative and at once informed any visitor of his interests and profession. I, of course, as a mere student of surgery, not only had limited funds with which to grace my humble rooms but far less prospect of finding anything with a professional theme which would be suitable for general view. I contented myself, therefore, with a charming photograph of my mother.

Luckhurst had been at college with Holmes, and we often discussed what our friend had been like in those days. I gathered that the man I knew was hardly different from the reclusive youth of former times. He had worked hard, often spending long hours alone with his books and papers, but rarely attended lectures. No-one quite knew the purpose and direction of his studies, which seemed to bear no relation to any formal syllabus, and which he never disclosed, least of all to his professors. I had once asked Holmes, out of curiosity, the nature of the degree for which he had enrolled, and he replied in such vague terms that all I could understand was what Luckhurst had confirmed — that he spent more time on his own individual pursuits than on the subject he was supposedly there to study. It was not therefore surprising that he had omitted to take his final examinations and left without a qualification before his three years were complete.

Holmes, said Luckhurst, had always displayed an enquiring mind but of a very peculiar and penetrating sort. He liked to mystify the other students with his deductions and then claim that he was exercising a simple skill that anyone with the right determination to train himself could achieve. This attitude did not win him many friends. The secret, he had once said, was to observe everything, even trifles. In fact, and this was a statement he returned to frequently, the trifles which were so often overlooked sometimes proved to be the most important details.

I could not help wondering what trifle I had overlooked in this strange and deadly conundrum of the Explorers' Club. Was there something I had seen or heard, which I had not realised was important at the time, and was allowed to rest forgotten in the back of my mind? Would this trivial fragment, if I could only remember it, be the key to the mystery? Whatever it was, I had failed to mention it to Holmes.

'Mr Rellish was not a hard man to find,' said Holmes when I next saw him, a few days later. 'I am fortunate indeed that he was not a Smith or a Jones, which would have taken me far longer. An examination of the recent Home Counties directories revealed that there is only one family of that name, and a brief correspondence confirmed that I had the man I sought. He is enjoying a quiet and bucolic existence as the curate of a small parish in Buckinghamshire. Rellish is a man wholly without ambition and I confess that I envy him his contentment, although not his means of achieving it. We attended the same university, though not the same college or years, but that and the fact that I had news of his former friends easily secured an interview, and I spent a very pleasant afternoon in his company.'

Holmes and I were in the students' reading room at the time, seated on either side of the fireplace and stretching out our toes to make the most of the meagre glow of coals. Those students who had been warming themselves before going to early suppers had departed, and we were left alone to speak freely.

Holmes painted a brief picture of his visit to see Curate Rellish, a comfortable sojourn spent before a log fire with clays and tobacco, while Mrs Rellish saw to the needs of three small children. 'He had been most upset to learn of the death of Bradstreet, of whom he had always held a good opinion. A man, he said, who had always led a good life, did his best to help others, and had not an enemy in the world. He thought that the tragedy was most likely to have been an accident, as he could not imagine what circumstances might have led such a man to destroy himself. I did not, of course, reveal my suspicions of foul play. He asked me to convey his sincere sympathies to the family.'

'Had he seen much of his old friends in recent years?' I asked.

'Hardly anything, as he had little in common with them and only rarely has occasion to visit the capital, something he tends to avoid rather than welcome. Many friendships formed in college do not continue once those days are gone and young men go out into the world to pursue their interests.'

Holmes, I knew, had few acquaintances from his college days, a fact to which he rarely referred, and seemed not to regret.

'I expect he wasn't able to tell you anything useful,' I said.

'Oh, he had a curious and amusing tale to tell,' said Holmes, with a chuckle. 'Human credulity in the face of greed is an extraordinary thing and never ceases to amaze me. What it tells me about the deaths of two friends and the disappearance of the third is something I have yet to determine.'

I gave the fire a cautious stir and settled to hear the tale.

'Rellish told me that the members of the college rowing team maintained their friendships outside of the sport, and they often spent time together in other pursuits and amusements. One afternoon, some of them were out in the town looking in those bookshops most favoured by impecunious students, when a paper fell from between the pages of an antiquated volume. Rellish could not recall who was examining the book at the time, or who picked up the paper. It was not necessarily the same individual. But the unexpected find did excite some interest, as it was thought possible not only that it was of some value, but that the shop owner had not realised it was there and had therefore priced the volume at an extremely modest sum. The paper appeared to date from the seventeenth century. It was penned during the wars of the three kingdoms; wars which ultimately led to the outrageous and indefensible execution of the King, and the formation of a commonwealth under Cromwell. It was most likely a fragment of a letter.'

'Did they purchase it?' I asked, wondering as I did so whether I might have been tempted had I found myself in a similar situation.

'There was some discussion as to the honest thing to do in the circumstances, with contrary opinions being expressed.

The rowing team may have pulled together when at the oars, but not, it seems, on other occasions. Ultimately, however, and by a majority decision, the paper was returned to the pages of the book, which was a translation of Ovid in very poor condition and thus of little value, and this was purchased for the original price asked.'

'I assume from what you have told me of Curate Rellish that he was not in favour of that action,' I said.

'He was not.'

'And Bradstreet?'

'He agreed with the majority.'

'Did the paper turn out to be very valuable?' I asked. 'Did they sell it? Was that the investment Bradstreet mentioned?'

'Their original intention was to sell, and they agreed to share both the cost of the purchase and the profit from the sale,' said Holmes. 'A closer examination of the paper, however, changed their minds, since it revealed an extraordinary story. The author was a staunch Royalist, who was writing to a relative, and it appeared that he was making plans together with some like-minded friends to conceal a cache of gold and jewels which they felt was in danger of being seized by their Parliamentarian enemies.'

'Really?' I exclaimed. 'How extraordinary! I suppose it would be too much to hope that the letter said where this treasure was to be hidden?'

Holmes smiled drily at my boyish excitement. 'Rellish could not recall all the details. He thought there might have been a name mentioned, but he was sure that there was no actual description of a place, other than that it was a secret location known only to the writer and his associates. In fact, he said that to him it sounded like something from an old storybook, and he gave it no credence, but to his surprise the other members of the rowing team seemed to take it seriously. It was the subject of careful examination and frequent debate.'

'For what purpose?' I asked, and then it suddenly became clear. 'Did they hope that the discovery might actually lead them to the treasure? Did they plan to try and find it?'

Holmes laced his long fingers and leaned back in his chair in contemplative fashion. 'It appears so.'

CHAPTER FOURTEEN

Buried treasure is indeed the common stuff of dreams and storybooks, but while it must be rare in reality, it is not beyond what is possible. 'How marvellous!' I exclaimed. 'Did they go? Did they find it?'

Holmes gave me a severe glance that quickly quelled my enthusiasm. 'As far as Curate Rellish is aware, they did not. It soon became apparent that such an enterprise would not be a simple matter. The paper as it stood simply did not have sufficient information on which to base an expedition. They were also aware that the undertaking might prove to be a lengthy and costly business. They needed to know more before they could make the attempt. They started to look for other papers; letters, wills, journals, personal histories and so on. Documents of that kind do come up for sale if they are of some antiquity and relate to notable families. These may be of interest to collectors and will carry some small value. But they would not be beyond the purse of a group of students if they pooled their resources. The rowing team therefore formed a joint resolution to gather information and meet up every so often to compare notes and buy up any papers of interest that came onto the market. They called themselves the Explorers' Club. If anyone was to ask about their meetings, they said that they were planning to travel abroad together after leaving college. Argento, because he knew something of the antiquities market, had some associates who dealt in old manuscripts whom he asked to keep a look out for relevant papers. Scordell, too, knew collectors amongst whom he made enquiries. It all had to be kept very discreet, and their ultimate purpose had to be strictly secret, as they believed that they were the only ones who were putting the pieces of the puzzle together. They feared that if their intention became known, the papers they needed which were of modest cost might suddenly acquire a much higher value, a price which would be impossible for them.'

I admit that by now I was thrilling to the high romance of this band of ambitious young men, when an unhappy thought struck me. 'Do you think it was this venture that formed headmaster Bradstreet's secret investment? His expectation?'

'I fear so,' said Holmes, 'and I must tell you that I share Curate Rellish's opinion on the matter. Rellish declared from the outset that he would take no part in the scheme, and he did not attend any meetings of the Explorers' Club. He knew that some of his fellow rowers were in need of funds to assist their future careers, while some simply liked the idea of pursuing a quest, but there were others whom he felt were only motivated by greed, which he deplored. Nothing about the scheme appealed to him. He did not like the hole-in-corner secrecy either, the decision that even close family were not to be told. All that he told me took place some years ago, of course, and he has heard no more of it since.'

This last comment led me to a sobering conclusion. 'I assume that given Bradstreet's failed promise to Miss Ellison and the state of St John's school roof, nothing has come of this enterprise,' I said.

'I am quite sure of that,' said Holmes.

'And was that the reason for Mr Bradstreet's despondency?' I asked. 'I can understand that it was something he was unable to share with his father or Miss Ellison, but he must have known, the other members of the club must all have known from the very beginning that success was far from certain.'

'If they did have doubts, they must have chosen to ignore them. Rellish, to his credit, did try to insert a little sense into the enterprise from the outset. He pointed out to his friends that even if this secret place existed, and they managed to locate it, they had to be prepared to find that no treasure had ever been placed there, or if it had, it had been discovered and removed many years ago, and all their efforts would be in vain. Even this did not deter them. He was assured that they were well aware of his objections, and they had agreed that if they located the site of the cache only to find that someone had got there before them, they had still made a useful investment as they would then sell the documents they had acquired which would have increased in value, and distribute the funds according to the amount each man had put in. It was therefore impossible for them to lose anything by the scheme.'

'That is something, I suppose. But it still doesn't account for Bradstreet's fear, and his warning message and murder. We know that both he and Geeson had been out of sorts very recently. Geeson mentioned betrayal by an old friend.'

'Yes, it appears that in the optimism of extreme youth the members of the club all seem to have decided to trust one another. That may have been a serious, even fatal error.' Holmes narrowed his eyes in thought and leaned forward, his thin frame hunched like a predatory spider. 'Let us suppose, for example, that Bradstreet had discovered that one of his friends had given the club's secret away and as a result someone else, who was not a member, had found the treasure. Assuming of course that there was any treasure to be found. Or perhaps he had learned that one of the club members had found it and kept it for himself and not told the others?'

'Both of those situations are possible,' I said, 'and both would result in distress, and I suppose even lead to murder, if large sums were involved.'

'But it is too soon to form any conclusion,' said Holmes. 'My mind remains open to all possibilities.'

'What about the other man in the rowing team, Bullstrode? Could Rellish tell you anything about him?'

'Bullstrode was a member of the Explorers' Club, but only briefly. Once he found he was due to be sent to Darjeeling, he told the others he would leave his small contribution in and hoped they would remember him if they were successful. I think we may discount him from any influence in the matter.'

'But Scordell was still a part of this, and he was a married man with a child on the way. If there is anything of value, his widow should have his share.'

'I agree.'

'Might Bradstreet have been murdered because of something he had discovered about this treasure trove? Supposing he had found where it was buried, and was killed to prevent him securing it for himself?'

'I do not discount that idea. But if he had discovered something, did he keep the information secret? If he needed extra hands for the work, he might have engaged the assistance of his most trusted friends Scordell and Geeson. But we get ahead of ourselves. All these suppositions rely on the proven existence of a buried treasure. I must ask myself this question: if, as Curate Rellish believes, we simply have some fanciful scheme by a group of students, a treasure that may no longer exist and papers which are not in themselves particularly valuable, then where is the motive for murder? Of course, Rellish does not know the current operation of the club. His story is several years old. The members continue to meet, and the status and operation of that association may have changed over time.'

'What can be done?' I asked. 'If there has been a murder which is not believed to be a murder, then the police will not investigate. And we are not detectives,' I added with a smile. Holmes gave me a hard look, from which I assumed that he considered his abilities far superior to any police or private detective. 'I don't believe Miss Ellison has the funds to employ a man to look into it. Old Mr Bradstreet might, but he would most likely be content if the coroner's court brought in a verdict of accidental death.'

'It is an interesting puzzle,' said Holmes. 'Why was young Mr Bradstreet murdered? What story do the documents tell? I would rather like to find out.'

'How do you propose to do so?'

Holmes chuckled. 'Oh, I have already taken steps. I have sent a letter to Mr Haxby at his club. I represented myself as a distant relation of a college man, who has heard the whisper of an Explorers' Club formed some years ago which is rumoured to have expectations. I have stated that I wish to join. I do not intend to name anyone as the source of my information. Not even Bradstreet, who although deceased might be suspected of telling Miss Ellison or his father whatever secret he possessed, thus placing them in danger.'

At that moment, our conversation was interrupted by one of the students. 'Oh, there you are, Holmes. You have a visitor; wants to have a private word. Looks respectable enough, but an odd sort. Do you know him?' He handed over a neat gilt-edged card. The name on it was Ruben Argento.

Holmes rubbed his hands together. 'And so the fish bites. Now we shall play him!'

CHAPTER FIFTEEN

Ruben Argento was waiting for us in one of the visitors' rooms. He rose to his feet a little awkwardly as we entered and for a few moments looked rather startled to see two men arrive instead of one, then he received another surprise when he recognised me.

'Oh!' he exclaimed, as Holmes introduced me. 'I remember you. I saw you give evidence at poor Bradstreet's inquest. You are the man who saw the tragedy happen.'

'I was,' I said, watching as a number of unfathomable emotions passed across our visitor's face.

'I do hope for the sake of his poor father that they determine that it was an accident,' he said at last. 'I cannot imagine what he must be feeling.'

'That does seem a very probable result,' said Holmes, blandly. He sat down, as did I.

Argento glanced back and forth at Holmes and me. 'The thing is, Mr Holmes, I hardly like to say it, but this is a very private matter, and I would prefer to speak with you alone. If Mr Stamford might consent to withdraw?' he added hopefully.

'Mr Stamford is fully acquainted with all that I know,' said Holmes. 'You may trust him absolutely. Please proceed.'

Neither of these assurances seemed to offer Argento any comfort. Reluctantly, he returned to his seat. 'My friend Mr Haxby has shown me the letter you sent to him,' he began. 'In it you referred to an association known as the Explorers' Club. Am I to assume that your information concerning that association came from the late Mr Bradstreet? How much did he tell you?'

'He said nothing about it to either of us,' said Holmes. 'I have no reason to believe he ever mentioned it to another individual.'

'Then before we say any more, I require you to provide the name of your informant and tell me how much you know,' said Argento.

'As to my informant, I am not at liberty to say,' replied Holmes, smoothly. 'All I have been told is that a club was formed some years ago when its members were at college, with the intention of purchasing documents which it was thought would in time lead to a valuable prize. It centred around a rowing team. Once I knew this, I examined the college yearbooks of the right period which listed the names of the team members, and naturally I recognised the name of Haxby, which is prominent in the banking world. Mr Bradstreet's name also appeared, as did those of the friends who gave evidence at the recent inquest.'

Argento uttered a sigh so deep that the expulsion of breath appeared to deflate his round body, and he sagged in his chair. 'How I wish the whole scheme had never been attempted!' he exclaimed. 'It has been nothing but expense and trouble without any result.'

'But the club still exists?'

He grimaced wryly. 'Oh, well, it does in a way. The members meet to dine regularly as we are old friends, but over the years the actual enterprise for which the club was originally formed has largely fallen into abeyance. I seriously doubt that it will ever amount to anything, and I have said so more times than I can recall. In fact, I have recently been trying to persuade the other members that the time has finally come to dispose of the few papers we have assembled and distribute the moneys amongst us.'

'Will there be a profit on the sale, do you think?'

'If so, I do not think it will be a large one. I had suggested that our collection should be valued by a reputable dealer, who does not know what we had hoped to accomplish. I have no expertise in that area myself; my interests are in Italian sculptures, glass, and ceramics. But there are several trustworthy dealers in London whose speciality is in books and documents. If necessary, we could have concealed our original purpose by dividing the papers between several men. But the members did not want our property placed in the hands of other persons. They feared, and I suppose rightly so, that experts do consult each other, and they might have compared notes. Then it was suggested that we simply make a general enquiry about papers of that age and condition, without revealing the originals. It was Geeson, Bradstreet's friend at St Paul's, who finally made the enquiry after we had all agreed on what he would say. The dealer he consulted would only go so far as a verbal statement, based on what he was told. He would put nothing in writing, for which he can hardly be blamed. The result was a figure which documents of that kind and antiquity in similar condition ought to make at auction, and it appears that after deduction of the usual expenses, we are likely to receive little more than the funds we paid out. It is a disappointment, of course, but hardly a tragedy.'

'And Geeson reported his findings to the club?'

'Yes. To us all.'

'Have the members agreed to sell?'

'I'm afraid not. I have tried to explain to them that after all this time, it is really the most sensible thing to do. There is no hope that our enterprise will ever meet with success. I believe that Curtis has begun to come around to my way of thinking, but the others would not consider it. I think they had become so enamoured of the idea of discovering a great prize that would make them rich, that they wanted instead to redouble their efforts. I also think they began to doubt my motives in trying to wind up the club.'

'In what way?'

Argento removed his glasses and pinched the bridge of his nose. As he did so, I saw that the gold ring on his little finger was in the form of a Roman coin. 'It was not expressly said, but I felt that there was a suggestion that either I had somehow already found the prize or had learned where it was and wanted to keep it for myself. I was actually being suspected of cheating them. It was rather upsetting, because even if I had found it, I would have shared it with my friends according to our agreement. But I am aware that some members are in need of funds which I am not, and will see our enterprise as a great opportunity, and be eager to continue. So, you see, Mr Holmes, I dare not suggest that another man be admitted into the club, as it would almost certainly be viewed with suspicion and strongly opposed. Neither do the members wish to have the papers sold, even if we have fair copies made for our information. They argue that so long as we hold the originals, no-one else can see or have them. We have kept our resources very secure indeed. Not that we have ever mistrusted each other, at least, not until now. We have always taken decisions by mutual agreement with voting if required, the majority to rule, and the principle of sharing has been sacrosanct. We have always protected our resources from those outside the club.'

Holmes appeared to be giving this statement deep consideration. 'Nevertheless,' he said at last, 'do you think there any possibility that the reason for the dissent, is that one of the other members has already found what you were all looking for and not shared it?'

Argento looked quite taken aback by the question. 'That is an idea I have not seriously entertained. None of the others has shown any evidence of sudden wealth. Far from it. Even if a member had acquired wealth and concealed it, there is another consideration. The location which we think is the one we are being pointed towards is sufficiently remote and hard to reach that even if we could precisely identify it, and we are a very long way from achieving that, it would require considerable time and effort to investigate, and, in particular, a prolonged absence from London.' He shook his head. 'No — I think not. I am sure not.'

I recalled that Bradstreet had left London in the summer, after telling Miss Ellison that he would be away for two or three weeks. Did Argento or the other members know that he had planned to be absent for so long? Had he gone in search of the treasure? Something must have occurred which had quickly put an end to that expedition and left him badly out of sorts on his early return.

At that moment, the door opened. To my surprise, three men entered, all of whom I recognised. They were the other three members of the Explorers' Club: Haxby, Tibbott and Curtis.

Haxby looked quite startled to see our little assembly, then became highly disgruntled. He pulled a large silver watch from his pocket, examined it, snapped it shut, and replaced it with slow deliberation. 'I recognise both these gentlemen,' he said, coldly. 'They were at the inquest on Bradstreet. I suggest that before we go any further, they should explain themselves and why they have taken such an interest in our private affairs, and most importantly, where they have obtained their information.'

'I don't think we should be concerned,' said Argento, quaking nervously under Haxby's stern gaze. 'I have explained that we cannot admit them to our club, and they understand that.'

'And yet,' said Haxby, squaring his shoulders in an effort to face us down, 'they seem to know far more than they ought, whereas we know almost nothing about them.' He fastened his gaze on Holmes with a sneer of disdain. In doing so, his face, which one might have called good-looking in repose, became curiously ugly. 'Are you a Jew?' he demanded. 'You have the nose for it.' Tibbott and Curtis tittered, although Argento, if he was also amused, kept it to himself.

'I am not of that faith,' replied Holmes, quietly.

Curtis thrust his thumbs into his pockets and stuck out his chin. 'They are just idle students,' he said, dismissively, 'playing foolish games as students will do. Pay them no attention.'

'We were once students,' Tibbott reminded him, 'and still are, in our own way.' He leaned against the wall in a casual manner, but his stance and look were alert.

'The truth now,' insisted Haxby. He paused by the fireplace, eyeing the fire irons as if he was about to pick up the poker to add weight to his demands. He caught Holmes' expression of utter fearless calm and thought better of it.

'We are indeed students,' said Holmes. 'My friend Stamford intends to qualify as a surgeon, and there are several professors who teach at the Medical College who will vouch for his good character. Myself, I am undertaking courses in chemistry and anatomy.' Holmes went on to give a good account of his college days in which he mentioned the Musgraves of Hurlstone, and the Trevors of Donnithorpe, as families whose sons he knew, and counted in his circle of friends. 'These gentlemen will confirm that it is my habit to engage in solving mysteries, mysteries which have dumbfounded others sometimes for many years, and that I do so solely for my amusement, and do not ask for or expect to receive any reward for my efforts.'

To my surprise, it was Haxby who listened to this information with more than the usual attention. At last, with some reluctance, he said, 'The Musgraves are a distant connection of mine.'

'A very old and well-regarded family,' said Holmes. 'I was at college with Reginald of the West Sussex Musgraves.'

'Here, we are not going to let him in?' demanded Curtis, belligerently. 'I don't care who he knows or what he knows; we have enough men in the club, and we don't want more.'

'Content yourself, sir, I withdraw my application entirely,' said Holmes.

'But wait a bit,' said Tibbott. 'Haxby, is it true that he solves mysteries?'

'I may have heard something of the sort,' said Haxby, grudgingly.

'Then we need to talk,' said Tibbott.

'I don't agree,' growled Curtis.

'I'm not sure I understand,' said Argento.

'Mr Holmes, Mr Stamford,' said Haxby. 'I feel it would be advisable for our members to meet in private for a discussion.' He glanced at the others. Tibbott nodded at once, and after a pause, Argento and Curtis gave brief nods as well. 'Depending on what we decide,' Haxby went on, 'you may hear from us. If you do not, then I would advise you not to approach us again. In any case, you are enjoined, as gentlemen, not to reveal to a living soul anything you may have learned of the Explorers' Club. It is something only the members may talk of amongst themselves, and you are not and will never be members.'

We gave our solemn assurances, and the meeting ended with the four visitors' departure.

'Did you know that the Haxbys are related to the Musgraves?' I asked.

'I recalled something of the sort,' said Holmes. 'One cannot have a prominent banker in the family and fail to mention it. It was not a cordial connection.'

'I can't say I took to Haxby,' I said.

'Blood is no guarantee of honesty,' said Holmes. 'You noticed, of course, from Haxby's manner and consultation of his watch when he arrived, that the gathering was intended to take place at an earlier hour and include all four of the members? I believe that Argento made sure to arrive before the appointed time to speak to us without the others present. He is afraid of something.'

'No one mentioned Geeson's absence,' I said.

'Quite deliberately, I think. Argento suggested that retrieving this treasure trove would require time, and Geeson has been away on a false pretext for weeks now. They are all thinking the same thing, that he has gone to find the treasure without revealing his intentions, but none of them would say it in front of us.'

CHAPTER SIXTEEN

I was at work in the chemistry laboratory two days later when Holmes burst in energetically, brandishing a letter. 'As I had hoped, Mr Haxby has written to Reginald Musgrave, whose membership of one of the oldest families in the kingdom — albeit of a minor branch — has been of little benefit to him but has proved to be a great one to me. His reply has confirmed that it was my habit at college to amuse myself by solving little puzzles and mysteries which had baffled both my fellow students and masters. Some of the students attempted to trivialise these successes, but there were others, and Musgrave was one of them, who took an interest in my methods, and were unafraid to pay me some quite gratifying compliments.'

'And Musgrave has recommended you to the Explorers' Club?' I asked.

'He has indeed. In fact, he went so far as to say that should he ever be faced with an apparently insoluble mystery, I would be the very first man he would consult. I will not say more, as it does not do to pay too much attention to one's praises which might lead to an undeserved confidence in my abilities. I am as liable to error as the next man, Stamford. Well, perhaps not the next, but the next but one. But I know it, and always strive for improvement.'

'Will you be admitted as a member of the club?'

'They do not go so far, and I will not press them. In any case, I do not think I require membership to learn their secrets. But I have been invited to take refreshments with them at the Mansion House Club tomorrow, when they have promised to reveal some small portion of their mysteries and will ask me to seek a solution.'

I very nearly begged him to take great care, but he knew the potential dangers, and as there were only four other gentlemen to meet, I felt sure that he could give a good enough account of himself if that was required, even if one of them did decide to arm himself with a poker.

'They required that you accompany me,' added Holmes, almost casually. I felt somewhat flattered by this until he added, 'They are well aware that you are in my confidence, and if they wish to keep a watch on me then you must also be included.'

I silently nodded understanding and then took to worrying if I had something in my apparel suitable for the occasion, as an invitation to a fashionable gentleman's club was rather out of my experience.

The following evening at six p.m., we ascended the old stone steps of the Mansion House Club and rang for admittance. Heavy double doors were opened, but these brought us only into a high-ceilinged anteroom, with a cool tiled floor and large pendulous lamps of brightly polished brass. We were met by a uniformed official, who made it clear that we were to proceed no further. He retired behind a breast-high desk made of ancient dark wood and produced a ledger the size and weight of an illustrious family's bible. With elaborate care he checked that our names were entered in that volume, and then, as we had finally met with his approval, he directed us in a manner that might have been accorded visiting nobility to a members' room on an upper floor.

We ascended by a broad winding staircase. The walls displayed portraits of former members, none of whom, from their expressions, appeared to have attained happiness from their pre-eminent position in the banking world. I did wonder briefly how much membership of such a club might cost, but as I looked around me at the size of the accommodation and quality of the furnishings, I realised it was not a question with which I would ever need to trouble myself.

The Explorers' Club had reserved a meeting room which was simply but luxuriously appointed. There was a long table, elegant chairs, and a sideboard provided with coffee, tea, water, baskets of cakes and savouries. A uniformed man could be summoned should anything else be required. After our first polite greetings, we were all seated at the table, and an order was placed for whatever drinks we preferred. Holmes simply asked for coffee to be brought to him and I thought it best to do the same, as I wanted to keep a clear head.

Haxby, as a member of the club, took his place at the head of the table, a position which showed he considered himself to be the leader of the group. No-one sought to upstage him. He leaned back in his chair, casting an openly suspicious look first at Holmes, then me, then back to Holmes again. At least he didn't make any suggestion of attacking us, so I thought we were safe.

'So,' he said, 'here is the position. As you already know, the club has a collection of documents. They are kept on these premises, in one of the private lockers which are made available only to members. It has been agreed by the members of the Explorers' Club that we will show you just one of our papers, and you will study it here, in front of us all, and let us know your deductions. You will not be permitted to copy it or remove it from the premises. Once you have examined it, it will be returned to its locker for safekeeping. Based on what you are able to tell us today, the members will then decide if you will be permitted to see another paper at a subsequent meeting. We also require that anything which is said inside this room and anything you see will not be revealed to anyone not of our fraternity. Should you reveal any details of our business, we have the power to ensure that you are never again regarded as a gentleman of honour. Those are our terms.'

I half expected Holmes to object. What if he needed time to study the paper? Collectors of antiquities could spend many years examining mysterious artefacts, and still not be able to identify them. Even after the discovery of the Rosetta Stone, it had taken several years to decipher Egyptian hieroglyphics. How might Holmes be expected in the course of a single evening to throw new light on a conundrum which had occupied the minds of the members of the Explorers' Club for so long? The demand did, on the face of it, appear to be far from reasonable. I glanced at Holmes, but he appeared unconcerned. 'I accept your terms,' he said. I think Haxby, too, was expecting an objection and was a little startled when none came.

'Very well,' said Haxby. He looked at the others. 'Shall we proceed?'

The other three signified their agreement.

The servant, a quietly dignified fellow in his sixties, arrived bearing our drinks on a silver tray. Everything looked so impeccable that I regretted not having asked for anything from the members' bar. Holmes and I were provided with our coffees, and a tray of tempting-looking eatables was brought to the table with water glasses and a carafe. The servant bowed. 'Will there be anything more, Mr Haxby?'

'Yes, Briggs. We wish to see the strongbox.' Haxby produced a bunch of keys from his pocket, which I could see was attached to his clothing by a stout watch chain. He showed one of the keys with its fob to the servant, who bowed.

'I'll bring it right away, sir.'

He was gone for a few minutes, during which we helped ourselves to food and drink. Although I was too interested in the proceedings to have much appetite, I did attempt a small plate to accompany my coffee, as I was not sure when I would taste anything like it again. Holmes, I noticed, drank only coffee.

The servant returned, bringing with him a small, stout metal strongbox, which he placed on the table in front of Haxby, then retired soundlessly from the room.

'This box,' said Haxby, laying his hands upon its sturdy lid almost reverentially, 'is the exclusive property of the Explorers' Club. It is our practice to take it in turns to hold its key. Tibbott, I believe you currently have the key?'

'I do,' said Tibbott. He produced a bunch of keys from his pocket and held it up to the members to display the smallest one, which was solidly well-made. The box was passed from hand to hand down the table, and finally it rested in front of Tibbott.

'Then please unlock the box. You must take out the top paper only and pass it to Mr Holmes, then close the box again,' said Haxby. 'You understand, of course, Holmes, that we of the Explorers' Club are all well acquainted with the content of the papers. We are looking to you to enlighten us with a new appreciation of their meaning.' Haxby's tone displayed a confidence he did nothing to conceal; he did not expect Holmes to enlighten the club at all.

Tibbott unlocked the box with great care, as if it was a fragile and sacred object. He opened the lid. For a moment he was silent, then his face furrowed into an angry frown and his head jerked upwards. 'Which of you has done this?' he demanded. 'Is this supposed to be a joke? I am not amused by it.'

'Whatever do you mean?' exclaimed Haxby.

Tibbott, growing more furious by the second, lifted the box and turned it about, tilting it so everyone at the table could see the interior. There was a strangled gasp of protest, which became a groan of dismay. The box was empty.

CHAPTER SEVENTEEN

The other three members of the Explorers' Club were out of their seats in an instant and ran to examine the box. Holmes and I wisely remained where we were. I glanced at Holmes, who was resting his chin on softly clasped fingers, a smile playing about the corners of his mouth. Curtis seized the box and turned it upside down. Haxby snatched it away and prodded and delved into its corners, tapping smartly on the base and sides. Then it was Argento's turn, and he shook it until the lid and hinges rattled. The box remained stubbornly and resolutely empty.

'Might I be permitted to look?' asked Holmes at last, as the distraught club members leaned on the tabletop, staring at the box, each one wrapped in his own private misery.

'Yes, do as you please,' said Haxby, with an angry gesture.

Holmes drew the box towards him and examined it with great care, both inside and out. Then he took his magnifying glass from his pocket and subjected its every surface to close scrutiny.

'Well?' said Haxby.

'It is a simple plain box with a single compartment,' said Holmes. 'Not only does it appear to be empty, but it undoubtedly is. There are also no signs of the lock having been picked or forced. It was therefore opened with a key. Before I proceed, please advise me of the procedures adhered to regarding the holding of the keys to both the locker and the strongbox.'

'The Mansion House Club lockers are a service only available to its members,' said Haxby. 'Each locker has only two keys.

As a member I have one of the keys, and the Club has a master key. Our strongbox also has two keys. One is held by the members of the Explorers' Club, who take it in turns, and the Mansion House holds a duplicate in its safe on our behalf.'

'Mr Tibbott,' said Holmes, 'please give me the key you have just used.' Tibbott glanced at Haxby, who gave a curt nod. The key was detached from the bunch and passed to Holmes who, after careful examination, used it to lock and unlock the box. 'As I thought, the key you have used is original to the box. It is an excellent fit and operates smoothly. But I can see some very fine abrasions around the exterior of the keyhole. At some point which I cannot of course determine, this box has been unlocked either by someone whose hand shook, or with a copy key which was not a perfect fit. It would require the services of a locksmith to examine the interior surfaces of the lock to determine which of those instances is correct.'

'What I want to know,' said Haxby between gritted teeth, 'is who has done this thing?'

'When was this box last opened that you know of?' asked Holmes.

'It was some weeks ago,' said Argento. 'Which one of us held the key then?'

'Geeson,' said Tibbott. 'I know it was him because it was he who passed it on to me. This is the first time the box has been opened since.'

'Geeson!' snarled Curtis, thumping the table with his fist. 'I always knew there was something not right about him. He was always too quiet, too ready to agree to everything. He thought he would fool us, but he didn't fool me!'

'Would Geeson have a locker key?' asked Holmes. 'Is he a member of the Mansion House Club?'

'I am the only member,' said Haxby. 'And I have never lent my key to Geeson or to anybody else for that matter.'

'But you have said that the Mansion House has a master key,' said Holmes. 'Would one of the servants oblige someone he knew to be a regular visitor by opening a locker for him?'

'There is only one way of finding out,' said Haxby grimly, ringing for the servant.

Briggs appeared soon afterwards. He looked about him, noting the change of atmosphere in the room, but said nothing. He looked unflustered, and was, I thought, quite used to the vagaries of young gentlemen, especially ones who were partial to spirits. 'May I assist you, sir?' he asked.

'Yes, Briggs,' said Haxby. 'We are all familiar with the protocol, here, that I demonstrate my membership of the club and possession of a key to a private locker, then you open it with the club's master key and bring me the strongbox. But tell me, have you ever opened any private locker for a man who is not a member, but simply the guest of a member?'

'Why, no, sir, that would be contrary to club rules.'

'Does anyone other than yourself open the private lockers?'

'Some of the members do prefer to use their own keys; that is, of course, permissible. There are two other senior attendants who also open them at the request of accredited members. I have never in my thirty years of service here known anyone contravene the rules.' His eyes had lit on the empty box, but he refrained from mentioning it. 'If I might ask, sir, do you have a complaint about our procedure?'

'What we want to know,' said Curtis, who appeared bitterly frustrated by the gentlemanly tone of the proceedings, 'is have you or any of the other attendants been asked to open the locker by our associate Mr Geeson? We ask because the contents of our box have been stolen!' he added, thumping the table for emphasis.

'We don't know they have been stolen,' said Argento, mildly.

'Then where are they?' demanded Curtis. 'Who has them?'

'I don't know, but what I meant was, they might simply have been borrowed.'

'Is there any action you wish me to take, sir?' asked Briggs, calmly addressing Haxby.

The members all looked to Haxby, who drummed his fingers indecisively on the table.

'If I might make a suggestion?' said Holmes.

'Yes, yes, go ahead!' said Haxby.

'I suggest that Mr Briggs, from his wealth of experience, should be asked to make careful enquiries and report his findings back to you before any action is taken. If, as Mr Argento has suggested, the material has simply been borrowed, then it may be returned shortly, and no harm done.'

Haxby glanced round at the others. No-one disagreed. 'Yes, Briggs, do as our guest has suggested, but this is a delicate matter and should be treated with delicacy. If anyone else, anyone at all, should ask to open the locker and retrieve the strongbox at a time when all our group are not gathered together, you must let me know at once.'

'I will do as you say, sir.'

Holmes returned the key to Tibbott, who re-locked the empty box. He handed it to Briggs, who bowed and retired from the room.

'And now what do we do?' said Curtis. 'And before anyone says any more, it is obvious to me what has happened. Geeson is the culprit! He has found some way of stealing the papers, and he has gone to act upon their instructions.'

'Since I have no knowledge of what these papers say,' began Holmes, carefully, 'I must ask if they point to a very specific course of action which would enable you to discover where you believe Mr Geeson might have gone?'

'I thought it was family troubles that caused his absence,' said Argento. 'Is he not in Lincolnshire?'

'That was what he told his employers,' said Tibbott. 'But I would wager that if we were to ask his family about him, we would find out he was not there and never had been.'

'But our papers do not provide us with sufficient information to act upon with any confidence of a quick success,' said Haxby. 'We only know that the reward we seek is at a very remote location, far from here. None of us have the leisure for a lengthy expedition, none of us has ever undertaken such an enterprise, and I doubt that Geeson has the funds to finance it alone.'

'But it is possible,' said Tibbott, 'that Geeson, being a librarian, and having some knowledge of and access to old manuscripts, might have lighted on something new, which for him has completed the picture, and instead of sharing it with us, as we all agreed upon, he has taken it on himself to go after the prize.'

'Has anyone seen him in the last month?' asked Curtis. Everyone shook their heads. 'No? Well, I have had my suspicions of him for some time, and this confirms it. I went to his lodgings last week and the landlady said that he was away, and a friend of his from the library had been there asking after him, too, so even his employers have begun to wonder what he is about.'

I glanced at Holmes to see if he would mention our conversation with Nevins, but he was silent.

Haxby glanced around the table. 'Gentlemen,' he said, 'we need to decide what to do next. We will await the result of Briggs' enquiries, but I wish to receive suggestions from the members as to what might be done in the meantime.' The Explorers' Club discussion was about to move into areas which were not to be shared with outsiders, and there was nothing for us to do but finish our drinks and depart. Before we left, Haxby grudgingly thanked Holmes for his attendance, and said he would let him know if there were any new developments.

'You didn't seem surprised at the papers being missing,' I said to Holmes, as we descended the steps to the lamplit street.

'I was not,' he said. 'In fact, I had expected something of the sort. That was why I was so ready to accept their conditions. At least one member of the Explorers' Club does not want me to see the papers, and I suspected that they would be abstracted for a while.'

'Then you think they will be returned?'

'That depends on who took them.'

'You didn't tell them what we had learned from Nevins,' I added.

'A little knowledge is a dangerous thing,' he said. 'And the time may have come when Mr Nevins will be useful.'

CHAPTER EIGHTEEN

Whatever Holmes was planning to do following our meeting with the Explorers' Club had to be postponed, since the next morning he received an interesting invitation. Miss Ellison had written to him asking if we two could pay a visit to Mr Bradstreet senior. She had apprised the bereaved father of her conversation with us, and Holmes' kind offer to assist in bringing some clarification to the tragedy.

'In view of our solemn promise, I will not of course be able to reveal what transpired at the Mansion House Club,' he said, regretfully. 'But I will do what I can, and I hope the father will be able to provide some information. He may yet know something of importance without realising what it is.'

'If Bradstreet and Scordell have both been murdered, I can think of no other reason than this secret hoard of valuables,' I said. 'Men have been killed for far smaller reward. It was meant to be shared between eight, but even if Bullstrode returns from Darjeeling, he will not have a large claim, and now two men are dead, and one is who knows where. Do you think one of the remaining men is murdering his friends one by one to increase his share?'

'If he is,' said Holmes, 'he knows not only where the treasure is, but what it is worth — knowledge that seems to have escaped the other members thus far. At least, that is their claim. Our criminal is a cold-blooded individual if he is prepared to murder old friends for money. But such things have been known. Dr Palmer of Rugeley, for example. He consigned a racing associate to a protracted and horrible death from strychnine solely to rob him so he might pay his debts.

Men have poisoned their wives and wives have poisoned their husbands for the value of their insurance, or simply to conceal their own depravity.' Holmes set his mouth and tilted his noble head to the heavens. 'It is a vile world, Stamford, and I must do what I can to make it a little less vile.'

Mr Andrew Bradstreet's house was a small, narrow and rather solid edifice with two storeys and a basement, nestling in a quiet portion of a Metropolitan suburb. The curtains were closely drawn, and a wreath hung gloomily on the front door. We were met by a weary-looking servant, a woman of middle years clad in the dark stuff gown of a general housekeeper, who showed us to the parlour.

A house of mourning always feels empty. There is a strange silence, the sense of a space forever waiting to be filled, and all around there are pendulous black ribbons and bows blossoming like new growths of dead flowers. Mr Bradstreet sat heavily in his bewilderment, with hardly the energy to rise and greet us. Miss Ellison, who was altogether sprightlier in her manner, had adopted the role of hostess to our gathering, and promptly ordered a tray of tea.

The house was genteel and orderly, with many mementoes of Mr Bradstreet senior's former occupation, framed testimonials and a little silver plaque, his retirement gift. We learned that he was a widower of many years standing, undemanding in his requirements and general mode of life. His son had led a similarly orderly existence. Frank Bradstreet had had his own rooms on an upper floor, which included a desk where he'd managed his affairs and correspondence. Apart from the necessary examination of his papers, nothing there had been moved or changed or disposed of since the headmaster's death. We were advised that the body was due to be released for the funeral once the inquest had reached its verdict. I did not expect to be sent an invitation.

The servant, transformed by activity if not garments into a maid of all work, brought a tray of tea things and some biscuits, but no-one showed any signs of having an appetite. Miss Ellison quickly dismissed her and set about pouring the tea.

'I am grateful to you gentlemen, of course,' said Mr Bradstreet, 'although I am not at all sure what you can achieve in this dreadful business.'

'I am not sure myself,' said Holmes, 'but I have an open mind and am willing to examine all the circumstances. It does not do to arrive at a conclusion until every fact, every possibility has been thoroughly investigated, and I feel that there is much work still to be done.'

'You may ask us anything you wish, Mr Holmes,' said Miss Ellison, warmly. Her eyes were the brightest thing in the room as she pressed a cup of tea into his hands. 'We will do all we can to help you, even if it pains us.'

'Can you tell me anything about the gentleman who is coming from Scotland to give evidence at the inquest?' asked Holmes.

Both Miss Ellison and Mr Bradstreet were unable to enlighten us. 'No, I cannot imagine who that might be,' said the unhappy father. 'We have no family connections or friends in Scotland. I have never been there, and I am sure that Frank never has.'

'Your son did spend a few days away from London quite recently,' Holmes reminded him. 'Might he have gone to Scotland?'

'I regret that I have no information at all about where he went. He told me almost nothing of his intentions. And this story he told Miss Ellison about his doctor advising him to take a holiday — I am sorry to say that I have discovered it is quite untrue. I asked our family doctor about it, but he told me he has not seen Frank for some time and has given no such advice. I have been wondering if Frank had perhaps begun to feel unwell and thought he might be suffering from some kind of illness. Perhaps he wanted to consult a man privately without my knowing, so as not to make me anxious about him. It would be like him to spare my feelings in that way. If that was his intention, Scotland was a long way to go, although I believe there are many excellent doctors there. Perhaps this man coming from Scotland for the inquest is a doctor. That is all I can suggest.'

'The evidence of the house surgeon at Barts showed that your son was in good health. Did he have any reason to suspect otherwise?'

'As far as we know, there was no sign of any bodily disease. I did speak to the doctors at Barts, who reassured me entirely on that point. But if Frank had been overworking, and was simply lacking energy, he might have entertained the idea that there was something the matter, even if it was not so.' Mr Bradstreet sipped his tea thoughtfully, with no suggestion that he tasted it. 'But I was pleased to learn that my son was not addicted to liquor or opiates. Not that I ever thought he was, but I was extremely grateful to have it confirmed. People do talk a lot of nonsense.'

Miss Ellison offered him the plate of biscuits, but he waved it away. No-one else wanted one and she returned the plate to the tray untouched. 'I could not help wondering if there was another explanation for his visit,' she said. 'There might have been a secret in Frank's life. Something he dared not reveal to anyone. He might have made an unwise marriage when he was a student, and had a wife and family hidden away who were a drain on his purse. Perhaps he went to Scotland to consult a legal man who could privately sever that association. That would explain his delay in arranging our wedding, and the lack of resources.'

'We have all behaved foolishly in our youth,' said Mr Bradstreet, sternly, 'but I would stake my life on Frank being honest enough not to promise you marriage if he was not free to do so. And, I might add, no-one has come forward to make a claim on him, which, given the widespread reporting of the tragedy in all the newspapers, might have been expected. No, you must put that idea entirely from your mind.'

Miss Ellison looked quite offended at the curt dismissal of her rather romantic theory. I wondered if by imagining this scurrilous behaviour in her intended, she had sought to soften the blow of his death. She began to offer more tea. Her hands shook a little, and as a result she was noticeably more generous in refilling Holmes' cup than she was with mine.

'I was wondering, Mr Bradstreet,' said Holmes, carefully setting aside his brimming teacup, 'if there was anything in your son's papers which demonstrates any connection to or interest in Scotland.'

'If there is, I don't recall it,' said Mr Bradstreet, 'but then I have only just learned about this Scottish gentleman, and when I examined the papers, I was not looking for anything of that sort.' He paused. 'My son's effects are in excellent order. I would not object to your looking at them. Another pair of eyes might see something I did not.'

This, I realised, was exactly what Holmes had hoped for. We all left the little drawing room and mounted a set of dreary stairs to the upper floor, where Frank Bradstreet had once lived. There were only two bedrooms and the usual offices. We were shown to a small tidy bedchamber with a narrow bed. There was an alcove beside the fireplace, furnished with a writing desk, before which stood a chair backed and seated with well-worn brown leather. Some shelves had been fitted above the desk and these held several books of historical or literary subjects, some of which Holmes established had been brought home by the father from the headmaster's office at the school, as his son's personal property. They included a bible, the Webster's dictionary, and an atlas of the British Isles. A single connecting door led to a small dressing room, with clothes, a washbasin and jug, and some simple toilet articles.

Holmes drew the curtains aside, although the small windows let in scant light, and began with a general survey of the rooms before directing his closest attention to the items they contained. He looked inside the small collection of books for any marginal notes or markings, but the atlas he simply balanced on the desk on its spine and carefully allowed the covers to fall apart naturally to show where it had most often been opened. It lay before us, displaying a double page showing a map of Scotland.

CHAPTER NINETEEN

'You say your son had never shown any interest in Scotland?' asked Holmes.

'No, none,' said Bradstreet, bewildered.

Holmes passed his magnifying glass over the pages but shook his head. 'He has not marked the atlas either in ink or pencil, but —' he leaned forward and his nostrils quivered — 'I can detect a slight scent.' On a thought, Holmes went to the little dressing room and returned with a pot of hair cream, which he opened and waved under his nose. 'Lime cream,' he said. 'Your son used this?'

'Yes,' said Bradstreet, sadly.

'I discerned a slight odour of it on the page, perhaps from his fingertips.' Holmes addressed himself to the atlas once more, lifting and tilting the book, scanning every inch of the open pages with his glass. 'There are some very faint marks, mainly on the edges of the pages as one might expect, but I can also see some tiny spots in the region of the Scottish islands, as if his fingertips have rested there.'

'Surely he cannot have gone there!' exclaimed Miss Ellison.

'If he was only absent three or four days, then I think that is hardly possible,' said Mr Bradstreet. 'And what possible business can he have had there?'

Holmes did not disagree. 'May I look at the papers in the desk?'

With the father's permission, Holmes undertook a thorough examination, which produced no new information. He then went on to look at the desk itself, crouching down to stare hard at the interior of some of the compartments. Taking up a ruler, he used it to compare their depth, then he inserted his long fingers into one of the compartments and felt his way around. 'This compartment on the left is shallower than its equivalent on the right,' he said. There was some more careful delving and then we heard a soft click. 'Ah, as I suspected. It is a common feature of many such desks. Well, we will see if we have found a prize.' After a few more moments of exploration, he gave a little cry of triumph. 'Yes, we have something which may be of interest.' Holmes withdrew his hand, and he was now clasping a small notebook between his fingertips. He took it to the window to examine it in better light.

'I cannot imagine what that might be,' said Bradstreet. 'It might not even be my son's; perhaps it was left there by a former owner of the desk. Is there a name on it?'

'No,' said Holmes. He swung about to face Mr Bradstreet, holding open the pages of the book. 'But I think this is your son's writing.' I could not help uttering a little gasp. The pages were covered with closely written numbers, and although I could not interpret them, they bore the same arrangement as the note which the headmaster had sent to his friend, indicating in groups of three a page, column, and word.

The unhappy father went quite white about the face when he saw the pages. He gave a groan and staggered back. Miss Ellison ran forward to take his arm and guided him to the chair, which he almost fell into. 'Oh, it is his!' he cried. 'I know the writing! I cannot deny it! But I do not know what it means, and I don't wish to know.' He reached out his hand imploringly. 'I beg of you, Mr Holmes, for the good memory of my poor son, we must consign this miserable document to the fire where it surely belongs!'

I understood at once what his fears were. A man who keeps what might be a journal in a secret code in a compartment known only to himself, must have something to hide which he does not want the world, or his family, to see. It wants little imagination to conclude what the distraught father must have feared. I glanced at Miss Ellison, but her mouth was set in a line, almost of triumph, as if her worst imaginings had just been vindicated.

'Mr Bradstreet,' said Holmes, gently. He went to his side and knelt by the chair, the better to address him. 'Allow me, if you will, to take this notebook away with me. Let me see if I can solve its mysteries. I would also like to borrow the dictionary, which I feel may be of use. I know how such a document must appear to you, but it might well throw some light on the circumstances of your son's death.'

'Some things are better not known!' he cried. 'Let my poor son rest in peace, with his good name intact.'

'I make you my solemn promise,' said Holmes, 'that if I am able to decode this writing, and if it includes anything which a father would not wish to hear, I will destroy all trace of it. But it might not be anything to distress you. What if, for example, it referred to the investments which your son hoped to realise in order that he might marry Miss Ellison?'

'Oh!' gasped that lady, and she cast herself to her knees at the stricken father's other side, taking his hand, so he was now flanked by the two supplicants. 'Yes, Mr Holmes may be right and there is nothing in it to be ashamed of. This might be the very thing we have sought, the record of Frank's secret fortune!'

'Is it possible?' asked Bradstreet, raising his head, a new glimmer of hope smoothing his features.

'I think it is very possible,' said Holmes, 'although I cannot assure you that any fortune will amount to a great deal.'

'But how — how will we know? How can we make any sense of these numbers? What do they mean?'

'If you would entrust me with this book, then I will be able to answer those questions,' said Holmes.

'Oh, please do!' begged Miss Ellison. 'Mr Holmes is so very clever!' As she said this, she turned her eyes towards Holmes, and I saw a light in them that had not been present before.

And then the realisation struck me that Miss Ellison, who seemed to have made a quick and substantial recovery from her disappointment in Frank Bradstreet, had taken something of a shine to Holmes.

Mr Bradstreet took a deep breath, nodded, and patted her fingers. 'Very well, my dear. I think we do owe it to Frank to look into this matter. Of course, there will be nothing to impugn his memory, and I am ashamed now that I even thought of it.'

Holmes and Miss Ellison both rose to their feet and brushed dust from their clothes. Miss Ellison took Mr Bradstreet's arm, assisted him down to the parlour and ordered more tea. The more I noted her looks and behaviour, the more certain I became of her feelings. Holmes, for his part, appeared to be quite oblivious to this development, which might seem a little strange for someone who prided himself on his powers of observation. On reflection, I decided that he probably had observed it, and had determined to ignore it utterly.

It was suggested we remain for supper; indeed, Miss Ellison was very earnest in her request, but the frown on the servant's face as the invitation was extended to us demonstrated how she felt about the unanticipated demands on both her services and the pantry. Holmes politely and firmly declined, saying that he wished to set about his important task as soon as possible.

We took our leave. As we returned to the City, I decided to mention my little observation. 'I think you ought to know that Miss Ellison —' I began.

'Miss Ellison is a disappointed spinster approaching thirty and desperate to be married,' Holmes interrupted brusquely. 'She will be engaged before six months have passed and will thereafter be no danger to anyone but her betrothed, but I cannot yet say whom that might be.'

I fell silent.

Some years after this revelation I read Watson's history of his friendship with Holmes, in which he said that Holmes had an aversion to women. I thought this put it rather too strongly. It is true that Holmes never sought out the company of women and felt more at ease either alone or with solely masculine companionship. He addressed women with outward courtesy yet always remained emotionally aloof. There were some rare individuals he admired for their courage, intellect and resourcefulness, but this did not impel him to get to know them better. Female beauty was not beneath his notice, but he regarded it as a snare to the powers of judgement, and he often spoke disparagingly of men who had been diverted from the paths of honesty and achievement or even brought to ruin by an attractive face.

'What do you think the notebook contains?' I said, changing the subject of our conversation and determining never to return to it again. 'There are several pages of these numbers.'

'Yes, and judging from variations in the ink and pressure of the nib, these notes were compiled piecemeal over a significant period of time. I would not be at all surprised if they relate to the mysterious papers which have been stolen from the strongbox at the Mansion House Club.'

CHAPTER TWENTY

I did not see Holmes all the following day, but it was not hard to deduce how he might be occupied. I next saw him in the chemistry laboratory on the morning of the resumed inquest on Frank Bradstreet, and he informed me that his decoding of the headmaster's secret notebook had been completed. 'It was based on the old Webster's as before, but I did at one point experience a small difficulty when the results, which had begun as I expected, suddenly started to make nonsense. However, I persevered and before long they began to make sense again. Then I saw that the stream of apparent nonsense could be interpreted simply by taking the first letter of each word. By so doing it yielded proper names, the only words which could not be found in a dictionary. I am now sure that these notes were based on the contents of the papers collected by the Explorers' Club. It is probable that they were not precisely copied word for word, which might have been tedious to achieve, and unnecessary. Bradstreet merely extracted what he deemed to be the essential information.'

'But how was he able to do this when he was not permitted to remove the papers from the Mansion House Club?' I asked. 'He could hardly have sat there writing out a copy while all eyes were on him.'

'No, but I do recall his father commenting that he had an excellent memory. I think that each time he saw the papers he memorised as much as he could of the salient points and then went home and recorded them. Over a period of time, he was able to assemble an account that would be useful in his quest.'

'And are these notes enlightening?' I asked.

'Yes and no, in that I can see the reason for and the object of the quest, but as we have been told, there was nowhere near enough information to clearly identify the location and thus make an expedition worthwhile. I doubt that anyone would have set out on a long journey simply on the basis of what he had learned from these papers.'

'The others thought that Geeson might have stumbled on something new.'

'I intend to look into that possibility. That is where Nevins will assist me. If you are not too occupied, you may join us,' he added casually.

I was by now used to burning a little midnight oil to catch up on my reading after Holmes abruptly demanded my company, and naturally I agreed. I doubt that my adventures in Holmes' company, which were always educational in their own way, occupied more of my student career than many of my contemporaries spent on less sober entertainments. But my eventual qualification as a surgeon must speak for itself. As ever, I surmised that Holmes did not require my presence because of my observational or deductive skills, which were far inferior to his. He often ruminated on problems alone, over a pipe or two, or even three, but sometimes it assisted his examination of a mystery to speak his thoughts aloud to another person who had shared his experience. Watson proved to be the ideal companion for this exercise, and I did well enough in my time.

'I have to admit I am extremely curious to know what Bradstreet's notes have revealed,' I said. I saw him hesitate for a moment. 'Even if you don't show me the result, anyone who knows you have them will assume that I have seen them as well,' I said.

'That is true,' Holmes said, and passed me his notebook. 'Disjointed fragments, as you see, but these fragments, whether valid or not, may have cost men their lives. I am no historian, but I have spent some time studying the background to these papers which, as I had thought, relate to a period of considerable unrest shortly after the wars of the 1640s.

'In 1649, the unthinkable, the unimaginable happened. King Charles I, the anointed sovereign, was tried for treason and executed, leaving his eldest son Charles as heir. In Scotland, ardent royalists rallied behind Charles II but the victories in battle of Cromwell's army crushed all hopes of a restoration of the monarchy, and the young king fled abroad in 1651. It would not be surprising, therefore, if some of the king's supporters decided to conceal their valuables from Parliamentarian troops.'

I began to peruse the notes. As Holmes had stated they were piecemeal, but I gained the flavour of them. He had listed them in what he felt sure was the order in which they had been written.

Item 1

1651

Dear brother,

Hard times will follow, but we will prevail. The new King is safe in exile and we pray for his return and restoration.

Battle against Cromwell lost. Many dead at Worcester. We must do all in our power to preserve our lives and possessions. Gold, silver, jewels. The value is great. The men of Parliament must not have them.

We will choose a hiding place known only to us. Others may join us. Trusted friends loyal to the rightful king. Seek those who will help our enterprise. We must dig deep and keep the secret. Make all secure. Mark the spot carefully. We will return to claim all when peace is in the land and King Charles restored.

Hugo

Item 2

Dear brother,

The place is chosen. Far north. Island to the west. Seen from promontory known by a horse head rock. Nesting seabirds. Dangerous precipice. No man goes there now.

Can row from shore. Old castle with single tower by cliff path. Much ruined and abandoned.

It will meet our purpose.

William

Item 3

Our men are ready.

We go by night.

Tell no one of our plan.

One rowboat will carry us all.

We meet by the horse head rock. A path descends.

Bring what is needed.

All will be safe.

Item 4

It is done.

All is hidden.

Buried by castle wall.

Our secret mark placed on wall above third stone from base.

Dig below mark two feet from wall, four feet down to find chest. Stout oak with iron bands.

Item 5

Bushes planted on the place to hide burial. All secure.

Be sure to keep secret, even under torture. Cromwell's men pursue us.

God save the King

Death to tyrants

Item 6

McClartondale treasure

Old Scottish family, loyal to King Charles I

Brothers Hugo and William planned to secrete family valuables after the defeat of Scots royalists in 1651.

They chose a ruined castle. It had once been occupied by an old branch of the family but was long abandoned. Only a single tower remained, on small island, off the west coast of North Scotland. The tower top could be seen from a promontory on the shore which resembled a horse's head.

Treasure was buried by castle wall. Carved into the stone above the place was emblem of the McClartondales, a prancing horse.

Soon afterwards both brothers, known to be ardent royalists, were taken prisoner by Cromwell's men, and sent to West Indies, where they died of fever. They never revealed the place where the treasure was buried. The secret died with them.

In later years after the restoration, their sons searched for the treasure, guided by some fragments of papers they had found hidden behind some wall panels. They believed they had discovered the island where the treasure was buried but found that terrible storms had lashed the coastline. The horse head was broken, the island cliffs had crumbled, and most of the old tower was swept into the sea, its secret markings lost. Only stones remain.

To this day the treasure, which may still lie in the earth, has never been found.

'It is clear to me,' said Holmes, 'that the first five items purport to be fragments of letters, probably all of them between the two brothers. The last, however, is a history, the work of another, which is unfortunately undated. Without the original papers, of course, it is impossible to be sure of anything.'

'So the McClartondale family were Scottish royalists who buried their treasure to protect it from looters in 1651, but the men who buried it never came back to claim it,' I said. 'And the Explorers' Club believe it is still hidden and hope to find it.' I tried to picture in my mind the map of Scotland in Frank Bradstreet's atlas. 'There must be a great many Scottish Islands.'

'Hundreds,' said Holmes. 'Most are uninhabited. You see the difficulty? The Explorers' Club must gather more information to establish which island it is that hides the treasure, otherwise it could take a lifetime and considerable expense to locate. The horse head promontory has been altered by storms and might be unrecognisable. If the cliffs and much of the tower have gone, then most of the clues could have been lost. And they need to act without alerting anyone else as to what they are seeking. Even if the history of the treasure is known to others, it may be that the club is in possession of the only firm clues to even contemplate a search. But they must also face the possibility that in the last two hundred years, someone else has forestalled them.'

'And the value of the papers?'

'They should be of historical interest and may be worth something to a collector. But if they point to hidden treasure, they may command whatever price an adventurer wishes to pay.'

'And a Scottish gentleman is coming to give evidence this morning,' I said.

'Yes. That should prove extremely interesting. I strongly suspect that he is not, as Mr Bradstreet suggested, a medical man.'

CHAPTER TWENTY-ONE

The stewards' office was more crowded than usual for what I think all attendees, but most especially the jurymen, hoped would be the final day of the inquest on the unfortunate headmaster.

Both Mr Andrew Bradstreet and Miss Ellison were there, and I also saw Alban Haxby arrive. The Explorers' Club had not come out mob-handed, which might have attracted attention, and I supposed that he was there to watch the proceedings on behalf of the members. I glanced around me in case the others should appear, and after a moment to two I saw Curtis slip into the room and lurk at the back.

'I don't think Curtis trusts Haxby,' I said to Holmes, indicating the new arrival. 'Haxby watches the inquest and Curtis watches Haxby.'

'Curtis trusts no-one,' said Holmes. 'His greatest fear is not lack of funds but a financial scandal. I have discovered that he is a minor secretary in government service, part of a small number who assist a member of parliament. It is a status he wishes to achieve himself. A share in a secret treasure trove might be very useful to his prospects, but if other interested parties should appear, descendants of the McClartondales, for example, and contested ownership it could damage his standing. Curtis joined the club's enterprise as an ambitious youth with the view of achieving wealth, but now he has started on the right path, he would not want to be associated with anything which could, if it became public, ruin his progress.'

Mr Payne opened the session with the observation that there was only one witness to be heard, after which he would be asking the jury to reach a verdict.

'I call Mr Henry Stewart,' said the coroner. There was a certain amount of interest in the room, as none of us had ever heard of this gentleman and even his appearance did not enlighten us. He was a refined-looking individual, aged about fifty-five, with grey hair and large eyebrows that gave him a searching look and the bearing of one who knew his business well.

'Mr Stewart, please tell the court about yourself,' said the coroner.

Stewart made a polite little bow of acknowledgement in the coroner's direction. 'I am a senior archivist of the National Library of Scotland, Edinburgh,' he said. 'I have a particular interest in the history of the earliest families of Scotland.'

'Please let us know why you have come to give evidence today.'

'When I read in the national newspapers about the unfortunate death of Mr Frank Bradstreet, I recalled that he had visited the library not long before. I do not know if his researches in Edinburgh have any bearing on his death, but wanting to be of assistance in the matter I wrote to the coroner's office and have come to tell what I know.'

'Please proceed.'

'On the 16 September last, Mr Bradstreet came to the library and made some enquiries. In view of the subject of his research, I decided to offer my assistance. He told me he was looking for histories of a Scots family called McClartondale.'

At this comment, I saw Alban Haxby's shoulders stiffen. Behind him, Curtis chewed his lower lip, an action which caused his ruff of whiskers to quiver.

'I asked him what his interest was in the family, but he declined to reveal it. He told me it was a private matter. I did not press him further. My experience is that when visitors come to make enquiries of this nature, it is often because they believe they have some connection to the family in question, that they might be direct descendants, or cousins. Often, they hope to have inherited land or a title. They are usually disappointed. But in such instances, they are always secretive, as they may fear attracting the interest of rivals.

'Mr Bradstreet asked to consult any personal family papers of the McClartondales, but I informed him that to the best of my knowledge there was nothing of that description deposited in the library or in any other. In fact, I was obliged to inform him that according to the official histories of the clans of Scotland, the McClartondales and their immediate kin became extinct many years ago. There is no-one of that name in our records after 1700. He made no comment on this, although I had the impression that he was not inclined to believe what I was saying.

'He then asked to see some histories and directories of Scottish castles. I was able to supply him with the volumes he required, which he studied very carefully, but without any satisfaction. He next asked me if the McClartondales had at any time inhabited a castle, and if so, might I advise him which one it was. From my own research, I was able to inform him that this was not the case. The family had occupied a farmhouse in the Lowlands, but poor harvests saw an end to this endeavour, and the house fell into ruin. Eventually and after some considerable effort, Mr Bradstreet was obliged to admit that his work in the library had not produced the results for which he had hoped.'

'Was he very despondent to realise this?' asked the coroner, pointedly.

'He was certainly unhappy. It is my belief that he had been looking to establish a valuable property right. I think he had come across some papers which had given him this idea. He had a little notebook with him, which he consulted often, although he was careful not to let anyone else see it. It was apparent that he was comparing the information in his notebook with what he found in the published volumes. At first, he appeared frustrated, and refused to believe what he was seeing there. When he finally accepted the truth and his hopes were dashed, he did become noticeably upset.'

'Did you, at any time, gain the impression that he might lay violent hands upon himself?'

'No, I did not. In fact, he stated that he must return home at once, as there were friends whom he urgently needed to advise of what he had found — or indeed, failed to find.'

'Is there anything else you wish to tell the court?'

'No, I think that is all.'

'Then you may stand down. If there is anything that anyone here present wishes to say, please advise me at once, otherwise the jury may now consider their verdict.'

Mr Stewart took his seat and since there were no further witnesses, the jury decided to retire to another room. While we waited, I saw Mr Bradstreet senior go to speak to Mr Stewart. Miss Ellison joined the conversation and appeared to be urging something onto them both. Eventually, Mr Bradstreet approached us. 'Mr Stewart will be returning to Edinburgh tomorrow morning, but he has agreed to dine with us as I wish to speak with him further. If you are not otherwise engaged, we would be pleased to have your company.'

Holmes accepted at once, and it was agreed.

'I don't suppose,' said Mr Bradstreet, quietly, 'that you have had any luck in decoding that strange notebook?'

'My work progresses,' said Holmes, 'but it would be as well not to mention it at present. I can inform you, however, that it contains nothing scandalous, and was related to the subject of your son's research in Edinburgh.'

'Well, that is a great relief,' said Bradstreet. 'I suppose in view of his expectations, he did want to keep them a secret until they had been realised. All the same, it is very strange behaviour indeed.'

The jury returned after twenty minutes and delivered an open verdict which satisfied no-one.

'Do you think Mr Stewart can help us at all?' I asked Holmes.

'I have no doubt that he can, but the question is, will he?' said Holmes. 'Did you notice that he was very careful to say nothing which impugned the reputation of Frank Bradstreet? The deceased was represented as an honest, earnest gentleman, who was merely in error. Often, the crucial content of a conversation is not what someone says but what he deliberately avoids saying. There is more, much more, and I mean to find it out.'

As we all filed out of the office, I saw Holmes approach Curtis, who was making an effort to slip away unobtrusively, and say a few words to him. Curtis gave him a surly glance but nodded. We found a quiet location for a private conversation.

'Have the missing papers been found?' asked Holmes.

'No,' growled Curtis, 'but I wasn't expecting it, none of us were. We think Geeson has them. If he can't find what we are looking for, he may try to sell them. He is best placed to know their value to dealers. I think he has been making enquiries he has told none of us about.'

'I know you can't tell me what the documents reveal,' said Holmes, 'and I will not insult you by asking, but I intend to keep my eyes open in case they are ever offered for sale. Could you tell me how I would recognise them? How many of them are there?'

Curtis stared at Holmes with smouldering suspicion in his eyes. 'How do I know you wouldn't buy them up and cheat us?'

'You don't, of course. You only have my word as a gentleman.'

'That's to be bought and sold nowadays.' He paused. 'Six papers.'

'And I think I can easily guess from the evidence we have heard today that they involve the history of the McClartondale clan? And date from the seventeenth century?'

'No hiding much from you, is there?' growled Curtis. 'One of them is a history, the others are parts of letters. That's all I am saying.' He stomped away.

Holmes ruminated for a while. 'As Mr Argento told us, the members of the Explorers' Club were prepared for a possible failure, so the dashing of their hopes of riches would have been a considerable disappointment, but not a shock. They were still left with the market value of the documents. Mr Bradstreet, however, from his financial position, will have had more reason than the others to be distressed at failure, but why did he feel the need to urgently tell his closest friends? Was there something else he had found, something unexpected? And was that the information which led to his death, and that of Scordell?'

CHAPTER TWENTY-TWO

The aromas of the dinner being prepared for us in the Bradstreet house were more redolent of the kind of simple catering thought suitable for students dining en masse. I sensed that many worthy foodstuffs had been boiled to destruction and the result would be edible and stomach-filling but not memorable.

Miss Ellison, devoting her energies to tending to Mr Bradstreet, was as prettily dressed as respectable mourning would allow, thereby showing herself off as the kind of feminine company, both pleasing and comforting, that so many men might have looked for in a wife. Holmes was almost determinedly unmoved by this and took care not to say or do anything which she might have interpreted as encouragement, although he remained as polite as ever.

It was not only the lady herself who did not engage his interest. Over the years I have known Holmes he has never once contemplated marriage, whatever the accomplishments, attractions, and connections of the ladies he encountered. Watson, who was something of a romantic, never gave up hoping that Holmes might one day be tempted. Holmes, however, had deliberately trained himself to be a pure thinking machine, a calculating engine, with no more idea of tender emotions than a set of cogs or wheels. Yet remarkably, his observation of emotions in others was acute and perceptive. He once, as Watson recorded in his account of *The Musgrave Ritual*, mentioned that a man could never appreciate that he had lost the love of a woman forever, however badly he had treated her. Coming from someone so youthful who had never had so much as a sweetheart, this was a remarkably incisive comment.

I believe that there was only one place he might have observed such a fault: his childhood home. Holmes never spoke of his parents, but he did sometimes muse on the idea of inheritance of character, and how a man might make a turn to the good or bad in his life depending on the instincts that descended to him by blood. Was this, I came to wonder, the reason for his turning away from any idea of marriage? Was there something in the relations of his parents that made him afraid that if he ever married, he would prove to be a bad husband, and cause pain to a good woman? I never dared to question him on this subject, and if Watson ever did, he did not record the result.

The company about the Bradstreet dining table was as serious and gloomy as the thin brown soup which began the meal. Mr Stewart, in response to the polite enquiries of his hosts, regaled us with the history and antiquities of Edinburgh, a city which he could not help believing was superior in every way to London. In the interval between soup and a dish of boiled ham and potatoes, Mr Bradstreet, who had been plunged into a silent reverie, suddenly said, 'I find I cannot believe, however hard I try, that my poor son ever imagined our family had a connection to Scotland or any family there. Did he never say what his reasons for this were?'

Mr Stewart looked troubled, and was considering how to reply, when Holmes said, 'You stated in evidence that many visitors to the library who make similar enquiries believe that they are related to a Scottish family. But I perceived that you did not say that Mr Bradstreet was of that opinion. Am I correct in deducing that he did not express this belief to you?

And that his enquiries were of a different nature which you did not place before the court?'

'I thought it only necessary to describe his research in a general fashion,' said Mr Stewart. He addressed himself to his bread roll and butter with more than the careful attention it merited. 'He came hoping to make a discovery and was disappointed. Surely that was all that was required by the occasion.'

'I don't understand,' said Mr Bradstreet senior. 'What else can be of importance?'

'I like to be apprised of all the facts,' said Holmes, 'and only then can I judge which are important and which are not. Mr Stewart, might I ask you, to begin with, about the notebook which Mr Frank Bradstreet brought with him? Were you able to glimpse the contents? Were they in the form of an essay in words, or a list of numbers?'

'That is a rather peculiar question,' said Stewart, 'but it was a series of notes as one might take in a lecture. There might have been some numbers included, such as dates.'

'And this material which he consulted so carefully, did you observe that when he compared his writings to the printed histories and directories which you showed to him, they did not match?'

'Yes,' said Stewart regretfully. 'It was obvious to me, from his increasing frustration and annoyance, that they did not.'

'Did you discover the reason for this?'

Stewart uttered a long sigh, and looked at Mr Bradstreet senior, who indicated with a nod that he was to continue. 'It was not a discovery, as such,' he went on. 'In fact, I expected it. You see, we have had visitors come to us on this very same quest before now. Oh, the last one was quite a number of years ago, but as soon as young Mr Bradstreet told me what he was seeking — in fact, as soon as he mentioned the McClartondale name — I strongly suspected what the situation was, and I was right. I said nothing about this at the inquest, as I did not want to say in public anything which you might have felt reflected on the good judgement of the deceased gentleman.'

A large platter of food was brought in and put on the table. It was hearty fare, and none of us felt able to tackle it, but assisted by a jar of pickles, brave attempts were made.

Holmes said nothing and Mr Stewart was silent again. I could see that he was waiting for the continuing permission of the father. 'Please go on with what you observed,' said Mr Bradstreet at last. He looked defeated, dejected. 'I suppose I ought to know the worst.'

'The McClartondales were not a wealthy family,' said Stewart. 'They were honest and hardworking, making the best living they could from raising crops. There was a smallholding not far from the coast, which they purchased, thinking it might be suitable for grazing sheep, and so they built a cottage there for a shepherd to occupy. But they reckoned without the weather in those parts, which could be violent and unpredictable. And the land they had come by was sold to them at a low price because unbeknown to them, it was being eroded by the sea, and so they built their cottage and sheep farm where they could not last. In a long night of storms, all was swept away, and they had nothing left but a jagged dangerous cliff. The farmland had to be sold, and they eked out their remaining years as tenants on what had once been theirs.'

'Then even if there were descendants, they could not hope to inherit anything,' I observed.

'Exactly so. But the story of the unfortunate family and the farm and the cottage that fell into the sea was something that lived on over the years. An author of Scottish tales, called

Rawlin Mackenzie, came across it and took the true story and embroidered it according to his own rather sensational tastes. He wrote a book, *A Romance of Old Scotland in the Time of the Wars*. In this book, the family, which he now called McClardale, were not poor farmers but wealthy royalists, the sheep farm became a remote island property and the shepherd's cottage the tower of an ancient castle. Two brothers, alerted to the invasion of Cromwell's army, determined to conceal the family valuables near the old tower, the top of which could be seen from a promontory on the mainland in the shape of a horse's head. They were captured and sent to the West Indies, where they died without revealing to their enemies where the treasure was buried. Many years later after the accession of King Charles II, their sons, having discovered some clues, went to the island to search for the family wealth, but found that both the tower and the promontory had been swept into the sea by storms and they could no longer locate the markers their fathers had left to direct them to where the treasure was buried.'

'When was this volume published?' asked Holmes.

'1833,' said Stewart. 'And yes, I did show a copy of it to Mr Bradstreet. You may think it was unkind of me to do so, but I thought it best to put an end to his fruitless search, which could only lead to more labour and expense. He went quite white with shock. I had the distinct impression that the wording of the story was almost exactly the wording of whatever material he had discovered and to which he was referring in his notes. Other men have also read this book and have guessed the origins of the story, and not a few have believed it to be a true history of the McClartondales with only the name of the family slightly changed. So you see, when a visitor to the library asks me about the McClartondales and starts studying directories of castles, I have a very good idea of what they are looking for.'

'Oh, my poor son!' exclaimed Mr Bradstreet, dropping any pretence of engagement with the dinner. 'I wish he had confided in me! At least it was all down to an honest mistake! I am only glad that there is nothing disreputable to his name.'

'Was this notebook found amongst his effects?' asked Holmes.

'No, I would recall something of that sort,' said the father. 'It was not in his papers here or in the material sent to me by the school. There was —' he hesitated — 'that other document.'

'I think that may prove to be a copy of the notes, made for safekeeping,' said Holmes.

Stewart glanced at us enquiringly, but no-one enlightened him, and he took the hint and made no comment.

Miss Ellison said nothing. I saw her lower lip quiver in repressed anger and decided that I would not want to see her in a temper. I felt sorry for her, too, of course. She had been promised marriage but asked to wait for a fortune that not only would never come but had never existed.

'And you say that no-one has come on that mission for some years?' asked Holmes.

'Yes, the last one was an elderly Edinburgh gentleman who was convinced that he was descended from the McClartondales, but he has passed away.'

The remains of the ham and potatoes disappeared back into the kitchen and were replaced with a shapeless grey pudding. Mr Bradstreet stared at it as if it was a tombstone. The application of jam did little to improve it, but we made the effort out of politeness.

Soon afterwards Mr Stewart respectfully took his leave, saying he had to take the early morning train to Scotland, and with rather less excuse we also decided to depart.

'I think,' said Holmes, as the railway carried us back to the city, 'we can be certain that when Frank Bradstreet returned to London after his research in Edinburgh, he shared what he had discovered with his closest friends in the Explorers' Club, the two men he trusted most, Geeson and Scordell. And the discovery was quite startling. Their quest had been for a mare's nest all along.'

'But what of the papers they had purchased?' I asked.

'Without seeing the originals, it is impossible to determine what they might have been,' said Holmes, although I could see that he was ruminating on them as we spoke.

'Perhaps,' I ventured, 'they were illustrations — drawings from the storybook, intended to look like old documents, which someone had cut out. They might have looked convincing to an inexpert eye. Perhaps they were extracted by someone who believed the story and had been on the same quest.'

'Whatever they may be, what we have learned today would suggest that they are essentially worthless. This means that all the members of the Club have lost their investment.'

'Although,' I went on, arguing against my own suggestions, 'Curtis said that Geeson was a good judge of old documents since he worked with them.'

'We are not in a position to speculate. Men can sometimes see what they want to see if it means financial gain. Geeson had risked his funds the same as the others, but I can see that if the error was exposed, they might have blamed him for leading them astray.'

'I wonder what happened to Bradstreet's notebook?' I asked. 'The one he took to Edinburgh?'

'That, I am fairly confident, was his notes of the salient points in the papers. He had translated the notes into code and hidden that copy in his desk, but the other he took with him to refer to in his research. Since it was not found in his effects, he might well have passed it to one of his trusted friends when they met after his return.'

'Geeson, perhaps? He might have used it to go on his own quest.'

'That is one possibility. But recall that Scordell asked Nurse Harmon about some papers as he lay dying. He seemed quite agitated about them. And burned papers were found in the basement near to where he fell. That might have been material given to him by Bradstreet.'

'Do you think he might have dropped the papers and fallen when he tried to retrieve them?'

'Possibly, although I suspect something more sinister. The papers were important, and he was sworn to keep them secret. He would only have taken them from his pocket to consult them or show them to someone he trusted. Who was the unnamed gentleman he saw in Gresham Street? It cannot have been a chance encounter, but most probably a meeting to discuss the papers. This man might have lured him into danger, and dropped the papers into the smouldering ruins, either by accident, or deliberately. He might even have set fire to them. When Scordell tried to retrieve them, he fell or was pushed.'

'But whom might he have trusted?' I mused. 'Although it strikes me that if he believed there was no fortune involved there was no need for secrecy, since there was nothing at risk. All had already been lost.'

'Why then did he take the matter further?' said Holmes. 'Why did he consult this gentleman he did not name? An expert in documents, perhaps? A detective? There is another mystery here. And it is a deadly one.'

'Are the sums of money lost by the members of the Explorers' Club really so great?' I asked. 'When they were students, they might not have been able to fund the enterprise to any great extent. In their later careers it might have amounted to more, but was it enough to provoke murder?'

'That is one fact I feel sure the members will not reveal to me,' said Holmes. 'But the papers are gone, and the Club is now little more than an association of diners and drinkers, all regretting their past errors.'

'Bradstreet was convinced that Geeson was in danger and tried to warn him,' I said.

'He was right to do so,' said Holmes. 'My next step, now that I know the name of the book in question, is to seek out a copy. If the British Museum Library has it, then I can confirm my suspicions.'

We had gone our separate ways before I realised that Holmes had omitted to mention what his suspicions were.

CHAPTER TWENTY-THREE

When I am working on my papers during a quiet afternoon when there are no lectures at college, I like to sit at home in my little parlour, with a nice fire crackling in the grate and a cup of tea at my elbow. On the day after our dinner with Mr Bradstreet I was thus engaged, and so engrossed that I was not aware of Holmes' footfall on the stairs or even that he had arrived to see me, until he knocked at the door.

He refused tea in a somewhat curt manner and threw himself into a chair. 'I am meeting Nevins to visit Geeson's lodgings in half an hour,' he said. 'Are you greatly occupied?'

I glanced at the heap of books, open volumes, pens, ink and writing paper on the table before me. 'No, I can leave my studies for a while,' I said.

He nodded and I began to tidy my materials. 'I examined Mackenzie's *Romance of Old Scotland* at the British Museum Library today,' he said. Something in his voice made me stop what I was doing and pay attention. 'My fears have been realised,' he went on. 'My enquiries confirmed that there had only ever been one edition of that volume, the one published in 1833. The letters and journals of the main characters are in the story, as is the history we have been told, but they are not in a form that could be mistaken for papers of the seventeenth century. They are simply printed as part of the text of the book. There are no illustrations, no inserts, and there never have been.'

I digested this momentous information. 'But the Explorers' Club believed their papers to be genuine old documents. How could that be? Pages cut from a printed book would not fool anyone!'

'No, and at least three members of the club had some knowledge of antiquities. But a child would know the difference between print and handwriting. I am sorry to say it, but there can only be one conclusion. The papers purchased by the Explorers' Club were forgeries based on the text of the book, which is itself a story. Who forged them and when and why, I have yet to discover.'

'That must have been what shocked Bradstreet and his friends,' I said. 'The realisation that for all those years they had not been searching for a real treasure. And it wasn't even a mistake. They had been deliberately duped.'

'I think that was the worst of it,' said Holmes. 'An error could have been put down to youthful folly.'

'Didn't Geeson talk of a betrayal? Could that be what he meant? If that had been me, I would certainly have wanted to make further enquiries, and find out the truth.'

'They may have done so,' said Holmes, 'and that could have ultimately led to the death of two and the disappearance of a third.'

'Do you think Geeson has been murdered?'

'It is one possibility. But I hope to learn more today.'

We met with Nevins in a cafe near to Geeson's lodgings. He had no further news for us, in that his friend had not reappeared at the library, and nothing more had been heard of him since we had last spoken. He told us that Geeson had occupied rooms suitable for a single gentleman in a tidily kept establishment about fifteen minutes' walk from the cathedral. 'The housekeeper is a Mrs Dawson,' said Nevins. 'She is a highly respectable woman, who stipulates that her lodgers must all be well-behaved young gentlemen, and I do not see any reason to suppose that Geeson did not meet that requirement.'

We were admitted to the lodging house by a well-starched maid and told to wait for the housekeeper. Mrs Dawson was a lady in her forties who reminded me somewhat of the senior nurses at Barts, since her manner suggested kindliness, efficiency, and an absolute refusal to tolerate any kind of nonsense. She greeted Nevins politely, and on being introduced to us submitted Holmes and myself to the kind of intense visual scrutiny ladies usually reserved for suitors making an application to court their daughters.

'I am sorry to trouble you once more,' said Nevins, apologetically, 'but I was hoping that you might have heard if Mr Geeson was to return soon. His employers are becoming extremely anxious about him, and my friends Mr Holmes and Mr Stamford have agreed to help me find out where he is.'

'I wish I could advise you,' said Mrs Dawson, 'but I have heard no more from him. His rent is due, and I expect I may hear something soon. He was always very punctual about his rent.'

'The fact is, Mrs Dawson,' said Holmes, 'that Mr Geeson told his employers that he had gone to see his family in Lincolnshire, but information has recently come to light to show that he is not there after all. In fact, we have reason to believe that he may be in urgent need of help. He may even be in danger. We are seriously considering consulting the police.'

'Oh, my word, surely that would not be necessary!' exclaimed the good lady. 'I can't have policemen in the house, what would the neighbours think?'

'It may not come to that, of course,' said Holmes. 'But if you might allow us to look over his rooms, a proceeding we would only undertake under your strict supervision, that might provide some enlightenment which would avoid such an inconvenient invasion. Perhaps he left a note for his friends to see, which would explain everything.'

Mrs Dawson hesitated. Nevins, she already knew slightly; we, however, were still strangers.

'My friends are students at Barts Medical College,' said Nevins.

The housekeeper's concern softened a little. She looked us over once more, and after a few moments, made her decision. 'Very well, but you are not to touch anything without permission, and I will require Mr Dawson to be there to see that all is kept in its proper place.'

She went to fetch a key and when she returned with it, she was accompanied by a tall, burly man with a glossy moustache who stared at us keenly and cracked his knuckles but said nothing. I could see why her lodgers were well-behaved.

We were conducted to Geeson's rooms, which were on the first floor. Holmes walked about the parlour and the bedroom, peering into cupboards and the wardrobe under the steely eyes of Mr and Mrs Dawson.

'Have you found anything?' asked Nevins.

'It is more what I have not found,' said Holmes. 'If Mr Geeson had intended to be gone for a month, he would have taken certain things, fresh shirts and linen, and other necessities. There are signs that some items of that nature have been taken. He keeps most of his possessions very tidy, but I can see some indications of disorder here and there which suggests that he made his departure in great haste. And there is no travelling bag. Did he have such a thing?'

'He did,' said Mrs Dawson. 'Brown leather with handles.' She looked about the rooms. 'It's gone. He was as good as his word. But you are right about his being in a hurry. He even cut himself shaving.'

Holmes gave her a curious look. 'Mrs Dawson, I can see that you are a very observant lady. I would be grateful if you could tell me as much as you can remember about the day Mr Geeson left. Who knows, it may all be a storm in a teacup. We may find him safe and well and he may even be home before the week is out.'

'Well,' said Mrs Dawson, 'I know it was a Saturday and a very fine day. And he said he was going out that afternoon to see a friend who wanted to watch some bicycle races. He'd had a note saying they should meet. A Mr —' she hesitated — 'Bradford or something like that.'

'Bradstreet, perhaps?' Holmes suggested.

'Yes, that was the name.'

'Where were these races to take place, do you know?'

'He didn't say. Only that he was worried the train might be very crowded. He was going from Liverpool Street.'

'Did Mr Geeson tell you then that he planned to go away?'

'No, not at that time. I don't think it was in his mind. I suppose he might have learned something from his friend that made him decide. I don't know. But when he came back, I heard him moving about in a very hurried way, which was unusual for him, and I thought I would ask if all was well. When I came in, he was putting things into his travelling bag. And he looked very upset. I asked him what the matter was, and he said he had witnessed a terrible accident, and was quite shaken by it. I asked if it was his friend who had been hurt but he said no, it was someone he didn't know, a lady. But he had decided to go away for a time, and he promised he would let me have a month's rent in advance. Then I saw that there was blood on his collar. I said to him, "Oh, Mr Geeson, you have cut yourself shaving" or something like that, and he didn't even know it and put his hand to his neck —' here Mrs Dawson put the flat of her left palm against her neck — 'and when it came away, it was all covered in blood. So I said I would wash his collar for him, as it would come out best while it was still wet, and he took it off and gave it to me. Then I think he went to see to the cut. I washed the collar as best I could, but when I came to give it back to him, he had gone. And there on the table was a month's rent in an envelope with my name on it.'

Holmes gave Mrs Dawson his card. 'If you should hear from him again, please let me know,' he said. 'And might I ask if you still have Mr Geeson's collar?'

'When it was dry, I put it in a drawer with the others, but I'm not sure he'll want it back.'

'May I see it?'

She seemed surprised but went to fetch the item. 'I don't think it's good for anything,' she said. 'There's a kind of burn on it.' She handed it to Holmes.

'Yes,' he said, taking out his magnifying glass and scrutinising a dark scorch mark. 'Mr Geeson does appear to have had a close brush with the fire. May I retain this? I promise I will let him have it back if I see him.'

'I don't see why not,' she said.

'I do have one more question,' said Holmes, putting the collar in his pocket. 'When Mr Geeson went out to see his friend that day, was he wearing his favourite yellow handkerchief?'

'I wouldn't swear to it, but I expect he was.'

It only remained for Holmes to examine a small collection of books on a shelf. With the housekeeper's permission, he extracted them one by one to look inside them. Apart from the expected Webster's dictionary and a bible, they revealed little more than a not unexpected interest in church architecture and history. At one point, with his nose in a volume of monographs about medieval bibles, Holmes gave a little smile, and I half expected him to make a comment, but he closed the book and replaced it on the shelf without a word.

We took our leave shortly afterwards. 'What was all that about the collar?' asked Nevins. 'What does it tell us, other than that he was in a hurry and leaned too close to the fire and then cut himself?'

'I can't say for sure at present,' said Holmes, 'but once I have a more powerful glass at my disposal than the one I carry about me, I may come to another conclusion.' Holmes would say no more, but I could see he was confident that he would have some news very soon.

CHAPTER TWENTY-FOUR

I had a full day of lectures the next day, and my evening was spent with my notes and books and a beef sandwich, but the following morning at Barts, Holmes sought me out. I think he was eager to find someone with whom he might share his discovery. He had deduced after a careful examination of Geeson's collar that he had not ventured too close to a fire or cut himself shaving. His neck had been grazed by a bullet.

'He said he had witnessed an accident to a woman,' I said.

'He did, and as we know the date of the accident, it was not hard to discover the incident he had witnessed,' said Holmes. 'Nevins, by a process of deduction, gave us the first date on which Geeson was unexpectedly absent from the library. It would have been the Monday following Scordell's accident, but prior to his friend's death. This means that the accident to the lady occurred on the previous Saturday. You will recall the list of unusual deaths that took place in the last few months and were reported in the newspapers. I had initially imagined that we were looking for a gang of desperate men and did not see any great significance in the unfortunate death of the carpenter's wife at the Alexandra Palace pleasure park. When there are public events held there, the railway company provides additional trains from Liverpool Street, which are often crowded. And Geeson was planning to take a train from that station. I do not congratulate myself on this discovery; it only strengthens my resolve to ensure that no detail, even one that appears to be unconnected, should escape me.'

'But the lady's death was a pure accident,' I said. 'A ricochet when a bullet missed the target and she just happened to be passing. No-one could have predicted or planned such a thing.'

'But what if the shot did not come from the range but only appeared to?' said Holmes. 'What if the would-be murderer was aiming at Geeson and the carpenter's wife chanced to walk across the path of the bullet? Geeson was unnerved, not only because he had witnessed a shocking death, but he must have guessed that the bullet was meant for him. That is why he fled.'

'The woman was brought in here,' I said. 'The inquest was held here. I remember the surgeons discussing it. But it was assumed from the start that the shot must have been fired from the shooting gallery.'

'Let us see what more we can learn,' said Holmes. 'We will begin with a more detailed examination of the newspapers.'

Fortunately, the newspapers we required were still in the reading room. We learned that the deceased, Mrs Esther Thompson, was forty-three years old, the wife of a master carpenter and the mother of five young children. One Saturday in September, the weather being fine and sunny, the family had decided to spend a day of amusement at Alexandra Palace where there were many attractions: bicycle races, swings and roundabouts for the children, and several shooting galleries. She had been walking with the children in the direction of the roundabouts, followed by her husband who was strolling only a few feet behind, and chanced to walk around the back of one of the shooting galleries, which was well patronised. The discharge of a rifle was heard, and she fell to the ground and lay there groaning. At first her husband thought she had fainted in fright, but then he saw blood streaming from her ear and realised that she had been shot. He summoned a cab and had her taken to Barts.

After reassuring himself that his wife was being cared for, Mr Thompson returned to the park and had urgent words with the owner of the shooting gallery, who said he was very sorry for what had happened. Together, they examined the precautions taken at the gallery. Behind each of the targets there was an iron plate, with thick wooden boarding on either side. The bullets were fired through an iron tube thirty feet long and one foot wide, the end of which was about eight or nine inches from the target. After striking the target, the spent bullets fell into a wooden box which was open to collect them. It was obvious, however, that despite the narrow line of fire enforced by the tube, it was possible to miss both the target and the iron plate. Several bullets were found embedded in the thicker boards, and there were also a few holes in the material comprising the structure of the gallery, showing that wider shots had passed right through. Mr Thompson said that he did not consider that the protection provided at the end of the gallery was sufficient. He thought that the bullet that struck his wife must have glanced off the inside of the tube and missed the target, the metal plate, and the heavier boards.

At Barts, Mrs Thompson's case was regarded as one of special interest to surgeons, who operated on the injured woman. Five pieces of her splintered skull had to be removed before the bullet could be extracted. Nothing more could be done, apart from making her comfortable and hoping she might recover. After lingering for three weeks, her condition suddenly declined due to blood poisoning, and she passed away.

The inquest was held at Barts, where it was pointed out that the back wall of the shooting gallery resembled the rear of a summerhouse and there was no notice of warning or any indication to passers-by of the building's actual use. The verdict was accidental death, but the gallery owner was ordered to increase the size of the targets and the iron plate, which he promised to do.

Holmes now determined to examine the medical notes. I think he was hoping that the bullet had been retained, but it had not. 'It was quite probably badly distorted, and I doubt that there would have been a way of showing what type of weapon had fired it,' he said regretfully, 'but I would have welcomed the opportunity to study it.'

Nurse Harmon, who had been so helpful to us before, had not been on duty when Mrs Thompson had been admitted, but she discovered the nurse who had attended the injured woman and brought her to us.

'The poor husband was in a terrible state,' she said. 'He kept moaning about his dear wife and his five little ones. He said the gallery owner was to blame for not making it safe enough, and there was a witness to the accident who he hoped would confirm it.'

'What witness was this?' asked Holmes. 'I don't believe any bystanders were called at the inquest.'

'He said that there was a young man standing behind the gallery very near to where his wife was walking. He was looking about him and waving a yellow handkerchief. He didn't know why. Then Mrs Thompson walked past and was shot. And the young man screamed. When Mr Thompson ran up to help his wife, thinking she had fainted, the young man cried out that she had been shot, and then he saw it was so.'

'Did he speak to the young man?'

'No, he must have run away in fright. When Mr Thompson came back after calling the cab, he had gone.'

'Geeson was already unnerved by what happened to Scordell,' said Holmes, when the nurse had returned to her duties. 'He must have thought the shot was an attempt on his life.'

'But I don't see how anyone can arrange for a bullet to be deflected in that way,' I protested. 'It had to be an accident.'

'I have shot at these galleries,' said Holmes. 'They are all constructed on similar lines. There is an opening at the side, a door leading to the interior at the back of the gallery which enables the attendants to enter when it is not in use if they need to adjust the iron tube or the targets. A man might enter unseen and hide there just beyond the line of fire to the targets and see out through a hole in the outer boards. He would have ample opportunity to sight his victim and take aim. The consternation that would follow such a shooting would be more than sufficient for him to make his escape.'

'That was the case at St Paul's,' I said. 'The reason Bradstreet's killer was able to slip away.'

'Precisely. Our man is extremely adept at making a murder appear to be an accident, and is neither seen himself, nor even suspected to be there. He is remarkable for his intelligence, imagination and coolness.'

Holmes appeared almost triumphant at identifying a criminal whose abilities made him a worthy opponent, and a suitable challenge to his own remarkable talents. I was terrified. 'Should the police be told?'

'And what can they do? Every fragment of evidence points to an accident. The inquest jury has spoken.'

'And Geeson, the only man who might support your suspicions, is missing and possibly dead.'

'Every mystery, every obstacle, is merely an opportunity, an exercise for the mind,' said Holmes. 'There are still avenues open that will lead me to the truth.'

CHAPTER TWENTY-FIVE

Holmes was not at the college the following morning, and naturally I had no idea where he was. Our previous conversation had left me concerned for his safety. I waited anxiously to receive the dreaded news that he was amongst the injured being brought into a ward or operating theatre or worse still, the mortuary, after suffering what appeared to be an unusual accident. I was therefore immensely relieved to see him later that afternoon, alive, uninjured and in exuberant spirits, demanding that I abandon my work in the library at once for an essential conversation. We found a secluded corner of the anatomy room, where the only other occupants were not in a condition to overhear us. We made a great show of studying some of the dissection charts in case anyone living should enter.

'You must recall,' said Holmes, 'when we spoke to Mrs Scordell, she described her husband's consternation when it was alleged that one of the exhibits at the art gallery where he was employed was a forgery?'

'Yes,' I said, 'but she didn't believe that had any connection to the Explorers' Club.'

'Neither did I, but at the time of that conversation I had not yet established that the papers collected by the club were forgeries. A month previously, however, after Bradstreet's visit to Edinburgh, where he was shown the *Romance of Old Scotland*, and told his closest friends what he had found, he, Geeson and Scordell would all have had their suspicions. Mrs Scordell told us that her husband had consulted an expert, a Mr Vambrook, regarding the gallery exhibit, but do you not think that he would have taken the opportunity at the same time to gather information which might enlighten him on the other papers, too? It was the ideal time to do so without breaking his promise not to reveal the business of the club.'

'Then we should go and see him,' I said.

'I intend to do so without any delay,' said Holmes.

'When is your appointment?' I asked, seeing yet another important lecture fall by the wayside.

'I have no appointment. I am going now. He does not expect my visit,' said Holmes.

This was rather surprising, but Holmes had that determined look about him, which deterred me from making any objection. If he was in so much of a hurry, I assumed he had good reason. My work in the library was almost complete, and I agreed to accompany him.

Holmes had obtained the address of Archimedes Vambrook from the London Post Office directory. He lived not far from Capital Fine Art in Brook Street where Scordell had once been employed. We found a wide thoroughfare lined with tall important-looking apartment buildings. These houses were the property of wealthy families, each serviced by a retinue of maids and footmen. The individual floors of the imposing edifices were sprawling homes occupied by the titled, the well-connected, and gentlemen of independent means, some of whom owned estates outside London, but liked to reside in the heart of society. For travel about the capital at a moment's whim, they kept their carriages and coachmen conveniently nearby but out of sight. We were less elegant in our approach.

We were allowed through the outer double doors to a reception hall, where Holmes explained our mission to the uniformed attendant. Holmes, I was pleased to see, had taken the precaution of obtaining a letter of introduction from Mrs

Scordell, saying that she had authorised him to make enquiries into the circumstances of her husband's accident. I am not sure if we would have gained admission to the collector's domain without it. Thus it was that a few minutes later we were conducted to the apartment of Mr Archimedes Vambrook.

We were met at the door by an immaculately dressed servant, in dark clothes and spotless white gloves. He examined the letter and requested us to wait while he spoke to his master. A few minutes later, Mr Vambrook came to greet us. He was only a little over five feet in height, aged between seventy-five and eighty, with the ascetic look of a dedicated scholar. His face was pale as paper, threaded by soft lines, with very bright blue eyes and a small thin mouth, and his hair was a series of elegant white curls clustered tightly to his skull.

'Gentlemen,' he said, in a welcoming manner. 'Your visit is unexpected, but I promise I will do all I can to assist you.' He conducted us to a large drawing room. 'Pray tell me how does Mrs Scordell fare? I know that she was in a delicate state of health, and her tragic loss must have seriously affected her.'

'She is bearing up well, with the support of her family and good friends,' said Holmes.

I could say nothing. I simply looked about me. We were in a room the like of which I had never seen before. To me, it resembled an art gallery or a museum, yet at the same time it was a warm and comfortable private home. The walls were lined in oak panelling, and there were handsome lamps carefully and sensitively illuminating the many works of art displayed there. I saw the glimmer of light reflected by oil paintings, the delicacy of drawings and etchings, all elaborately framed. The subjects were almost entirely religious, the Holy Family, biblical scenes, the crucifixion, and resurrection, and they were tasteful in the extreme. Other, secular portraits of dignified husbands and wives clad in heavy velvets decorated with delicate gold thread embroidery, were a tribute to old and respectable wealth. Below these pictures stood polished cabinets in which dozens of small sculptures and artefacts were arranged, and taller chests, towers of flat wide drawers with brass handles, which suggested a collection of documents.

A small and beautifully preserved writing desk was in one corner, and I guessed that Vambrook had been sitting working there when we arrived. A large chair had been pushed back and his pens, papers, spectacle case and an open ledger were where he had left them. He smiled as he saw me looking at it. 'The work of cataloguing is never done,' he said. 'New discoveries acquired, new material to enlighten me on pieces I already own. It is a blessed labour.'

He ushered us towards a richly upholstered antique sofa, before taking his place on a no less remarkable matching armchair. All the seating in the room looked to me like the kind of furniture set apart for occasional use by distinguished visitors, yet here it was, in daily use.

We were offered refreshments, which Holmes quickly declined on behalf of us both.

'How may I help you?' asked Vambrook.

'Mrs Scordell has informed me that there was an item in the recent exhibition of sacred art at Capital Fine Art, which was questioned after being sold, and that her husband, although not directly involved in its acquisition, consulted you about it. I am trying to learn something about his state of mind, and also what other research he might have carried out, the other people he consulted, and places he visited in his quest for knowledge. It is possible that these concerns, these actions, might have had some part to play in his unfortunate accident.

In particular, it might help to explain why he was in Gresham Street that day, something his widow is unable to explain.'

'Ah, yes,' said Vambrook, solemnly. 'Young Mr Scordell was a very serious gentleman, and a great devotee of art, especially paintings, although the questioned item was not in his area of expertise.'

'Please describe it.'

'It was, or purported to be, a page from a bible, apparently dating from the sixteenth century, and written in Hebrew. Items of that nature can be extremely valuable, both because of their age and rarity and their important contribution to our knowledge. They are eagerly sought after and collected by libraries, museums and scholars, and the best examples will command high prices. This item was acquired by the gallery from a highly reputable dealer, a Mr Berman, who has a shop in Canon Alley. Berman mainly deals in old books and papers, and from time to time he advises the executors of wills on manuscripts which form part of the estates of deceased collectors. In such accumulations one always finds an abundance of less valuable material, but the occasional treasure can come to light. This manuscript was thought to be such a find. It had an established provenance. It was purchased at auction and had been in the late owner's possession for several years. Berman does not purchase such valuable material himself, but he sells on commission for the executors.'

'How was it found to be a questionable document?'

'The purchaser first entertained suspicions when he saw that the content appeared to be at odds with other items in his collection. He had the document examined by a chemist, a leading man in his field, who determined that the material had gone through a process making it appear to be older than it was. It was not a recent repair to an existing document of the right age. The whole piece was suspect. He concluded that it was only a few years old, and a complete forgery. His opinion was not absolute proof, we can rarely have that, but it was enough for the gallery to admit fault and come to an arrangement.'

'I assume that Mr Berman was not held to be at fault?'

'Not at all. He conducted his business in good faith and was himself out of pocket. In the thirty or more years he has been in business as a dealer, there has never been a word against him; never any suggestion that he has forged or artificially aged documents. In fact, he would have been unable physically to do so, as he suffers from arthritis in both hands and has done so for many years. The penmanship of the forgery was exquisite. There is a workshop there where his father, who died some ten or twelve years ago, once carried out document repairs and bookbinding. Nowadays, he employs a young assistant for that part of the business.'

'Do you think Mr Scordell was content with the information you gave him?'

Vambrook was silent for a moment. 'I think he was, although after we had concluded that matter, the conversation did take another turn. He seemed very interested to know how forgeries, of old documents in particular, are carried out. He wanted to learn how someone like himself, with no expertise in that area, might examine a document in order to ascertain if it was genuine or not. I had the distinct impression that he was not thinking of the suspect document we had just discussed. Either he was expressing a general concern to assist him in his future career, or — and there was something very earnest about his manner that led me to suspect it — he had another specific document in mind. So much so that I asked him if he was concerned about something and suggested that if he was, he might bring the item to me, or I could go and see it and let him know what I thought, but he seemed embarrassed by the question and claimed he did not have anything in mind. I have to say I was not entirely convinced.'

'Do you personally know of anyone who is or has been suspected of producing forgeries of important documents, or who might have the skills to do so?'

'I do not. There are men in prison who have forged wills and bills of sale, but an antique document is quite another thing. To produce something which will convince men of learning who have made such material a lifetime study, that is a very refined and delicate skill. It cannot be acquired in a short time. It is something that would take many years of study and practice, trial and error.'

'Do you know why Mr Scordell was in Gresham Street on the day of this death? Did he ever mention that he intended to go there? Mrs Scordell has told me that the site of the warehouse fire was somewhere he would not have ventured by choice.'

Vambrook shook his head regretfully. 'It is a mystery to me.'

'When he was admitted to Barts, he told the nurse that he had met with a gentleman there. Can you suggest who that might have been?'

'I am afraid not. I wish I could be of more help to you, but I can throw no light on this dreadful affair. Please do send my good wishes to Mrs Scordell. Perhaps, when she is safely through her confinement, I might pay her a visit. A little christening cup would be an appropriate gift, I think.'

'There is one other thing you might assist me with,' said Holmes.

'I will do what I can,' said Vambrook.

'I would like you to produce Mr Geeson, who I believe is residing here.'

If it had been possible for Vambrook to become paler than he already was, he would have done so. He stared at Holmes speechlessly, and I saw fear and uncertainty in his features.

'Please do not deny it,' said Holmes. 'I imagine you met Mr Geeson at the library at St Paul's. I know you study there. You gave him a copy of one of your books, a collection of monographs on the subject of medieval bibles, in which you pay a generous tribute to the cathedral library, and you inscribed the gift to Mr Geeson, thanking him for his help. He came here for sanctuary. He is here now. The chair at your desk has been pushed back by a man very much taller than yourself, and I see a spectacle case, a small one for pince-nez, which I know he wears for reading. They leave a very distinctive mark on the bridge of the nose which you do not have.'

In the face of this train of evidence, Vambrook looked quite helpless.

'I understand your concern,' said Holmes, kindly. 'Mr Geeson believes that an attempt was made on his life by the same man who was responsible for the death of his friend Scordell, which was not, as it was meant to appear, an accident, but murder. He may well be correct. I also think that the same man murdered the headmaster Bradstreet.'

'Surely not!' exclaimed Vambrook, who had begun to tremble.

'I was at St Paul's that day,' I said. 'I saw Bradstreet fall. In fact, I am the only man who did. I am sure that he was deliberately killed. And if any man can bring his murderer and Scordell's to justice, it is Mr Sherlock Holmes.'

At that moment, the door opened and a figure appeared. It was not the servant, but a much younger man. He was tall and very slender, with a stooping posture, long hair, and a mild expression. 'I can't live in fear anymore,' he said, quietly. 'I will talk to these gentlemen.'

CHAPTER TWENTY-SIX

As Geeson stepped further into the room, I saw that he had the ghastly pallor of an otherwise healthy man who had not stirred outdoors for a month.

He sat down wearily. Vambrook gazed at him sympathetically and rang for his servant. Coffee was ordered and Geeson looked as though he needed it.

'I read about Bradstreet in the newspapers,' he said quietly. He gazed at me, eyes wide in sorrow and dread. 'You say that you were there? You saw what happened?'

I gave him my account of the event, which was essentially what I had said at the inquest. When the coffee arrived in a giant silver pot with enough cups for four, we all solemnly partook.

'Were you at the cathedral on the day Bradstreet died?' asked Holmes. 'He must have imagined he saw you on the gallery, which was why he went up there.'

'I was not there that day,' said Geeson. 'I was here.'

'I can attest to that,' said Vambrook, firmly. 'Mr Geeson has not stepped out once since he came here.'

'And the yellow handkerchief?' said Holmes. 'That was the reason Bradstreet thought it was you he saw. Do you have it with you now?'

'No. In fact, it might well have been mine or one like it,' said Geeson miserably. 'I lost it.'

'Mrs Dawson told us about your state of fright on the day you went away, and it was not hard to deduce that you were at Alexandra Palace pleasure park when that unfortunate woman was shot,' said Holmes.

Geeson looked surprised but nodded. 'I was.'

'Tell me about what happened. Had you planned to go there before, or did you decide on the day?'

'I did not plan to go there. I received a message from Bradstreet that morning,' said Geeson. 'He had recently taken an interest in bicycling which none of us thought to be entirely wise, given his old injury. He said he wanted to go and watch the races and would be pleased if I could meet him there. He was about to depart for Liverpool Street to catch his train, so I was not able to reply. I thought someone ought to be with him in case he was tempted to try and ride one.'

'You are sure the message was from him?'

'Yes, it was his writing, his signature.' There was a pause, then Geeson uttered a groan. 'I see what you mean. I'm sorry, but it never occurred to me that it might have been anything other than genuine. Foolish under the circumstances.'

'Do you still have it?'

'No, I don't keep my correspondence.'

'Go on.'

'The letter said it might be very crowded at the park, but he would easily find me if I stood near to the roundabouts and waved my handkerchief. I did as he asked, but I looked around and couldn't see Bradstreet. Then, that poor woman walked past me. I think she was guiding her children towards the amusements.' His hands were shaking, and he put down his cup. 'I think of that family often, those little ones! So happy, so innocent! Their last moments with their mother! I was trying to look for Bradstreet again, and just as I turned my head, I heard the shot. She just fell. Dropped to the ground like a stone. Her husband was not far behind, and he ran up, and said "Oh! She has fainted" but there was blood, and she was groaning, and that was when we knew she had been shot. There was nothing

I could do. I felt a sting on my neck and thought at first it was an insect. It was only later that I realised that the shot had grazed me. It was not that poor woman but I who was to have died. And then I thought of Scordell in hospital, and I had my suspicions about that, too. I am not a brave man, I confess it. I had to run away.'

'How did you lose the handkerchief?' asked Holmes.

'I'm not sure. I didn't have it when I got home. I must have dropped it, but I don't know where. In the train, on the field. The last time I remember having it was just before the shooting.'

'Who do you think tried to shoot you?'

'I don't know what to think. Bradstreet's letter had made me go to that place, but he might have written to others too. And now you think he might not have written it at all. But I didn't see anyone I knew. All I know is that someone wanted to kill me,' he ended miserably.

'Mr Geeson has had a very great fright,' said Vambrook. 'I had previously suggested to him that he might like to help me with the catalogue of my collection, and when he came here after his dreadful experience, I was happy to allow him to stay as my assistant. I thought the work would allow him to rest and recover his equilibrium. I really cannot imagine who might mean him any harm.'

I sensed a tender, almost fatherly manner in the old man.

'You have been kindness itself,' said Geeson to his benefactor. 'When I came here, I reassured you that I had not committed any act of even doubtful legality, and nothing of which I should be ashamed. My conscience is clear, but I have not told you all. My fault is that I have been too trusting, and now, since my foolishness has led to this, and I am no longer in danger of betraying any confidences, I think it is time for me to tell all.'

We listened attentively as Geeson embarked on the story that Holmes and I already knew, but Vambrook was learning for the first time; the college friends in the rowing team, the chance discovery of the first paper and others subsequently purchased, the formation of the Explorers' Club, the determination to find a treasure trove.

'Who first suggested the idea of messages in code?' asked Holmes.

Geeson was thoughtful. 'When we were all at college it was easy enough to meet and exchange information, but we did realise that when we left, we would become more scattered and would have to send letters. We talked about it, and I think the idea came from stories of spies and how they sent messages. There were some old dictionaries in a bookshop, and we bought their stock. We were young men, hardly more than boys, and to some of us, it seemed like an adventure out of a storybook which had been made real,' he went on, smiling sadly at this admission of folly. 'But now I fear that it was just a story after all, and the papers we had trusted were false. We had been keeping a secret that never existed.'

'And after so many years had passed without result, did any of the other club members come to suspect that the papers were not genuine?' asked Holmes.

'If they did, they did not say so. But I know that some had lost hope of finding the treasure. Argento certainly believed the papers were genuine. He wanted to have them valued by a reputable dealer, and then sell them and distribute the proceeds. Curtis thought the same. But Haxby still believed in the adventure; he wanted to go on, and so did Tibbott and Bradstreet. Bradstreet was in urgent need of funds. Haxby has always been eager for money, and the easier it is come by the better. And Tibbott — well, he is largely dependent on his father, who pays his gambling debts, but he knows that cannot go on for much longer.'

'And did you want to continue?' asked Holmes.

Geeson looked embarrassed. 'I — yes, well, Argento thought that selling the papers would not bring in a large sum. I have enough salary for a bachelor existence, but no more than that, and no other expectations.' I saw his face crumple a little. He must have been thinking of his family circumstances but did not enlighten us. 'And there is a lady I wish to court, and I have nothing to offer her.'

'Have you had these papers examined?' asked Vambrook. 'I would be glad to do so.'

Geeson shook his head. 'The consensus of the members was that no-one else should see them. It was agreed that before we even thought of selling them, some general enquiries should be made about their possible value. I was sent to consult a dealer about documents of that nature and antiquity and was told they might well have some value and be worth offering for sale.'

'Whom did you consult?' asked Holmes.

'My initial suggestion was Berman's, since his shop is in Canon Alley and I pass it when I go to the cathedral, and Mr Vambrook has spoken well of him, but when that name was mentioned, Haxby absolutely refused to consider it. He said some very harsh things about Berman. So I went to another shop on Cheapside. Barnett's, I think it is called. There was really nothing the proprietor could tell me with any assurance without actually seeing the papers.'

'I stand by my opinion of Berman,' said Vambrook, 'and I am sorry to hear that Mr Haxby is in any way involved in this business. There is an unfortunate history between that family and the Haxbys. Anything that young man says on the subject should be regarded in that light. I only know the story by rumour as the affair never came to court, and it was many years ago. But I have no reason to doubt it, given what I know of the Haxbys.'

We were all attention. Vambrook, on seeing our expressions, realised that we were waiting expectantly to hear more, and he had no alternative but to continue. 'Arnold Haxby, the father of Mr Geeson's friend, is a prominent man in the banking world. Some twenty or more years ago, he was out walking close by the cathedral and encountering a respectable young married woman of the Hebrew persuasion, he ordered her out of his way. She was with child at the time, and hesitated to comply, but he, caring nothing for her condition, roughly elbowed her aside, with an insult I will not repeat. She fell to the ground and suffered an injury which was not in itself very serious, but she lost the child and subsequently died. She was Berman's wife. He was left with three young children to care for. He made a claim against Haxby for his cruelty, but Haxby said it was an accident and his friends supported him. There was nothing Berman could do but make the best of it.'

'Haxby the son takes after the father,' said Holmes.

'So I have heard,' said Vambrook. 'But Geeson, tell me, how did you come to doubt the validity of the papers if no-one but your friends had seen them?'

'That was down to Bradstreet,' said Geeson. 'He was more eager than the rest of us to find the hoped-for prize. He wanted to marry, and the school was making demands which he and the trustees were unable to meet. Following my enquiries at Barnett's, Bradstreet feared that if the papers were sold, he would not receive nearly enough for his needs. He decided to make enquiries of his own. He told us he was going to Dorset for some sea air, but that was a lie. He had copied out the wording of the papers from memory, then knowing that the quest directed us to Scotland, he went to Edinburgh to find out more. We didn't know what he had done until he came back and asked to see me and Scordell very urgently. We met and he told us what he had discovered. The whole story of the treasure was a complete invention. There never was any treasure. He had seen a storybook written in 1833 and the papers we had, which were supposed to be much older, quoted that story directly. We were shocked, of course. It was hard to believe we had been fooled for so long. The thing that really concerned us was that it now appeared that the papers we had must be forgeries. Why would anyone do such a thing? I admit that I did briefly wonder if these papers might have been created in good faith to be used in a play based on the story and had somehow found themselves sold as genuine by mistake. But I never found any evidence that such a play had ever been performed or even written.'

'What did you tell the other members?' asked Vambrook. 'What did they say?'

Geeson looked mournful. 'We decided not to tell the other members until we had more facts. At the time, it seemed like the right thing to do. We even talked about the possibility that the papers might prove to be genuine. Perhaps, we thought, despite appearances, the author of the book had based his romance on real events.' He sighed. 'We were like drowning men clutching at straws. But we felt we had to be sure before we said anything. So we made a plan. And I have a horrid feeling that it was that very plan that led to the deaths of my two friends and the attempt on my life.'

CHAPTER TWENTY-SEVEN

Geeson refreshed himself with more coffee before he was able to continue. His face was drawn with grief. I sensed that the beverage had been his only source of sustenance for some time.

'We determined to proceed with caution. Ideally our aim was to be permitted by the club to ask an expert to examine one of the letters and assess it for genuineness. But this would never happen without the agreement of a majority of the members, which we doubted could be achieved. We were each assigned a task. I was to discuss the subject of how to prove the genuineness of documents with Mr Vambrook, whom I already knew through his studies in the cathedral library. But I was only to do so in relation to the medieval manuscripts, which were his speciality.'

At this, Vambrook nodded. 'I recall the conversation,' he said. 'Knowing what I now know, I can see you were most circumspect.'

'Scordell offered to speak to the other members of the Explorers' Club individually to discover their opinion on whether one document might be selected and submitted for expert examination. We hoped that this would lead to the question being put to another vote. Bradstreet said he would continue researching the story of the treasure in the British Museum library. We agreed to meet up again in a week to share what we had discovered.'

'I gather that Bradstreet was the most disappointed of you three,' said Holmes, 'and the most hopeful of being proved wrong.'

'He was. In truth, Scordell and I had long assumed that the entire thing would come to nothing, one way or another. Perhaps we would never find the treasure, or someone else would have got there before us. But after that first meeting, the day after Bradstreet came back from Edinburgh, I found that the more I thought about it, the more firmly I believed that an examination of the papers would find them false. The small hope I had clung to had only existed because I was reluctant to believe that for all those years we had been so cruelly, even deliberately misled. We had trusted each other, but that might have been unwise.'

'You have not told another person of the club's quest?'

'Not until today. I don't believe Bradstreet had either.'

'And you say that Scordell was intending to consult only with members of the Explorers' Club?'

'So he said, but his connections at Brook Street might have led him to cast his nets wider. I can't be sure what he might have revealed or to whom. Shortly before his accident, Scordell told me that he had spoken to a man at the gallery in general terms about whether documents are a good investment. He was told that it depends on the age and the author and the historical importance, but he was warned to be wary of forgeries. There are clever means of making a document seem older than it is, and only a great expert can tell the difference.'

'Do any of the members of the Explorers' Club have the skill to produce convincing forgeries?'

'Not to my knowledge. But a man might have been paid to do it.'

'Do you suspect anyone of having instigated the deception?'

'No. It might have started out as a harmless joke, but then when we all placed so much faith in it, the culprit, whoever he was, was too ashamed to admit to it. Perhaps he thought he would lose our friendship, our trust. He might even have enjoyed watching us all deluding ourselves and allowed it to continue. I don't think Scordell or Bradstreet would have acted in such an underhand way, and I know I did not, but there were nine of us on the team.'

'If you don't mind my asking,' said Vambrook, 'where are the papers kept?'

'They are under lock and key in a repository at a gentleman's club,' said Geeson.

Holmes and I exchanged glances. Either Geeson was an accomplished liar, or he had no idea that the papers were missing.

'If you had them in your hand now, what would you do with them?' asked Holmes.

'I wish I did have them,' said Geeson. 'I would show them to Mr Vambrook and ask for his advice.'

'But surely,' said Vambrook, 'the question of these papers is no more than a prank, and little has been lost and might easily be restored if the man responsible humbles himself with an apology? It is not a serious matter, like the document questioned at the Brook Street gallery.'

'Yes, that did weigh on Scordell's mind. He found it far more important than our small collection, and referred to it often,' Geeson admitted. He turned to us. 'A document had been displayed in the art gallery which was later questioned. The original owner had bought it five years ago. It was sold, but the buyer queried its genuineness. It was examined by some very accomplished scholars who found small errors in the lettering, and they arranged for an examination of the paper and ink under a microscope. The conclusion was that it was a forgery, albeit a very good one.'

'Mrs Scordell mentioned this to me and said that the gallery was able to come to a settlement with the purchaser,' said Holmes. 'Her husband, since he had not been involved in the original transaction, was not held to be at fault. The reputation of the business remained secure.'

'Yes, the art gallery compensated the purchaser and added a bonus for his trouble. Their main business is paintings, drawings and sculptures. They had not ventured into documents before and based on this experience may hesitate before they do so again. Scordell, as you have said, was not in any way to blame.'

'Yet you say that he continued to be troubled after the matter was settled,' Holmes observed. 'Why was this?'

'He pointed out that the document had lain unquestioned in a collection for five years. It was good enough to be accepted as genuine by all but the most expert eyes. He asked himself — had the person who made it only created one such item? When he thought about it, it seemed most unlikely. There could be others, many others. He feared that there had to exist in collections and libraries and auction houses all over the country, even the world, other false documents, just as good, or even, as the skill of the forger grew over time, almost indistinguishable from the real article.'

'In other words,' said Holmes, with that gleam of excitement in his eyes which I had come to recognise, 'we are no longer considering a few questionable papers of doubtful worth, which may have been no more than a student prank, we are looking instead at the work of a highly organised expert forger, a master criminal producing pieces which are thought to be extremely valuable and who has been operating with impunity for several years.'

He leaned forward, and I saw Geeson quail a little under the intensity of Holmes' stare. 'This is a very important question. Think carefully. Did Scordell discuss these concerns with anyone else apart from yourself and Bradstreet?'

'I don't know,' exclaimed Geeson, almost stuttering in agitation. 'He didn't say. He might have done, of course, with the gallery owners and their clients. But I wouldn't know their names.'

'Do you think he discussed it with Mrs Scordell?'

'I am not aware of that.'

'He did express some concerns to her about the affair of the document and the reputation of the business,' I commented, 'but I had the impression that he did no more than reassure her that he himself was not being held accountable, and his position was secure.'

'I tend to agree,' said Holmes. He turned his gaze towards Geeson again. 'But he did conduct meetings with Bradstreet and yourself, and the three of you took it upon yourselves to make enquiries in general terms about questionable documents and how to identify them.'

'Yes, but that was because of the papers held by the club, not anything else,' said Geeson.

'True, but your actual purpose was something you were all sworn not to reveal. If the master forger came to know of your meetings and subsequent enquiries, he would not have been aware of their precise subject. He might even have thought that you were on his trail.'

'Oh,' said Geeson, looking very shocked. 'Oh, I see.'

We all sat silently for a while, and I believe Holmes and I were thinking the same thing. Here at last was the answer to what had been puzzling us, the reason why a man might be impelled to commit murder. I couldn't put it into exact words, but I suspected that Holmes had the entire picture clear in his mind.

'He has kept his secret for many years, now,' said Holmes. 'The work of a master forger is easily concealed. It may be carried out in a single room. A study in his home, an artist's studio, or better still, a workshop apparently dedicated to an honest trade, such as bookbinding and document repair. Such a room would have all the necessary tools and materials he requires, and not arouse suspicion.'

'There are several such workshops in this part of London,' said Vambrook. 'I discount Berman, however. Berman's father might have had the knowledge and skill, but there has never been any suggestion that he was other than a plain hardworking journeyman, and he died many years ago. Berman, as I have said, cannot do work of this kind, and the young man he employs is barely twenty and does only simple repairs.'

'But a criminal might use a long-established business with a good reputation as a conduit for his work,' said Holmes. 'A screen for his own criminality. He might simply rent a workshop, by the day or the week, claiming to pursue a legal trade. His forged documents would then be offered for sale, with the appropriate papers, also forgeries, purporting to show a legitimate origin.'

'That is a possibility, yes,' admitted Vambrook. 'And that is very concerning. Many booksellers and bookbinders in London have Jewish proprietors. Barnett's too, although Mr Haxby was clearly unaware of it. If this scandal was exposed, then prejudice against Jewish businesses might mean that an innocent proprietor is accused of complicity in a serious crime which would result in a long term of imprisonment. I may appear English to you, Mr Holmes, but my family is from further afield, and we have had our unpleasant encounters with men such as the Haxbys. The English like to imagine that they are superior to all countries and all races on earth, but while they have much to be proud of, I believe that history has clearly demonstrated that for the finest scholars, artists, inventors, and men of medicine, we should look to eastern lands, which were far advanced in skill and knowledge when Englishmen were little more than primitives.'

I saw Holmes' eyes rove to the family portraits that hung in the room. 'I share your concern,' he said, 'but it goes further than that. I agree with Mr Scordell that these crimes have been committed over a number of years and may have been unsuspected until now. The forger has been alerted to the fact that he is in danger of exposure, which would result in a very long prison sentence. He may work alone, but he might also be only the tool of a larger criminal organisation, in which case if he is discovered, he will be a danger to them. Once arrested he could bargain with the law, hoping to lighten his sentence should his information lead to the apprehension of more powerful men. If this is the case, then he is very afraid indeed, and that fear has led him to kill.'

CHAPTER TWENTY-EIGHT

Before we departed, Vambrook provided us with the names of several businesses he knew which offered document repairs. Holmes had determined to visit all of them, his intention being to discover which might offer the best opportunity for a forger to pursue his work in secret. I was reminded of the time when we had trudged about the streets of London with increasing weariness, searching for the hired wagon involved in the curious case of the Rosetta Stone. I knew that Holmes would not abandon his quest until every avenue had been thoroughly explored. It went without saying that he anticipated having my company as an extra pair of eyes if nothing else. It was not, I thought, so much that he thought I might see something that he did not, but my presence established in his own mind the difference between an ordinary observer and an extraordinary one. As usual, he made use of the expedition to study the streets of the capital and its people and regaled me extensively on the minute signs which fed his remarkable powers of deduction. There was no opportunity, of course, to discover whether what he told me of places and random passers-by was true, but I was convinced that he was right in most cases.

Of Mr Vambrook Holmes had little to say, except that the unusual surname was most probably an anglicised version of the original Dutch. Based on the motifs he had observed in the family portraits, he thought the source of his fortune was diamond cutting.

After a while, however, he fell silent and I sensed that he was considering more deeply what he had learnt that day, especially concerning the Haxbys.

Sherlock Holmes, it must be said, was a patriotic Englishman through and through and he took it as read that the English were the finest race in the world. As a student of chemistry and anatomy, however, it would have been impossible for him to deny his enormous debt to the scholars of other lands and other races, and he never attempted to do so. In his efforts to explain how men behaved, he often mused about the descent of character by blood, and this encompassed not only the traits he had observed in families but those often attributed to nations. He had seen for himself that a good family might produce a villain and the reverse was also true. While a man's father might be a criminal and a blackguard, he might still manage to escape that dreadful inheritance or suppress the bad instincts with which he had been born and live a peaceful and honest life. Such was Holmes' theory.

He knew better than most that there was good and bad in all the world's peoples. Therefore, he judged those he met as individuals, and most importantly on how they behaved towards others, especially those placed lower in society than themselves. Above all, he despised arrogance and cruelty. I saw from his expression when we spoke to Mr Vambrook that he was appalled by the violence of Arnold Haxby's behaviour towards Mrs Berman. The assault had been based on nothing other than her race, sex, and position in society, all of which had made it hard for her to protect herself or protest. Had Holmes been present at that incident, I know he would have been the first to leap to her defence.

We browsed the bookshops, having little difficulty in appearing to be impoverished students looking for bargains. Holmes even made some discoveries which pleased him, and he was able to add to his collection of old volumes. Some of the shops only sold books and pamphlets. They did not offer repairs on the premises but when asked, the proprietors referred customers to another business nearby. Some businesses which did offer repairs did not have a separate workshop. There would be a little alcove at the back or to one side where a man bent over a desk, surrounded by the chemicals and tools of his trade, working in plain view of customers. Those booksellers that did have workshops often separated them from the areas where customers walked with a windowed wall. It was easy to glance inside and see one or two men and sometimes women quietly and patiently at work. We also looked for aged documents being offered for sale. We saw a few in poor condition, and old bibles badly in need of repair, but they were not priced at significant amounts.

Barnett's, the Cheapside shop where Geeson had made his enquiries, was a larger establishment than most, extending over two linked premises. One part sold new publications; books, pamphlets, and newspapers, and the other was well stocked with second-hand material. Both were well patronised. The trade of bookbinding and repairs was advertised by a poster in the window as being carried out to the highest standard by experts. Either this was being done somewhere on the premises which we were unable to view, or in a separate workshop. There were doors at the back of the shop, but these could have led either to workrooms or stores. The proprietor was a middle-aged man, with several assistants whom we guessed to be his wife, sons, and daughters-in-law. They occasionally conversed in a language I could not recognise, and which Holmes suggested might be German.

There were documents offered for sale, many in that spiky script known as Gothic, displayed handsomely in glass frames and with prices that were well beyond the means of a student. Behind the counter were tall, locked cabinets with the flat trays that suggested a substantial trade in that area. Holmes took his time studying what documents he could see, even taking out his magnifying glass. I wondered if the proprietors were accustomed to this kind of behaviour, but although they watched him with interest, they appeared unconcerned. At last, Holmes shook his head. 'I have not yet acquired sufficient knowledge of chemistry to come to any conclusion,' he said regretfully.

We stopped briefly to refresh ourselves at a cafe. 'Really, Holmes,' I exclaimed, 'I know that you have already deduced a great deal, and I would be obliged if you would share your thoughts with me.'

He hesitated, then said, 'Very well, let us see where we are at present. It is always wise to assemble events in the order in which they occurred, so revealing how one led to the next and so on.

'The Explorers' Club has been largely inactive for some time, or at least, for the purpose for which it was first established. The members meet to dine, and there is some lip service paid to the arcane and formal ritual of the opening of the casket and examination of the papers, but no real effort has been made to chase after this elusive treasure. Most of the members were not in immediate need of funds, apart from Mr Bradstreet. With the approach of the winter season, the demands of the school roof had become more pressing, and I strongly suspect that Miss Ellison had begun to hint about planning a spring wedding. At the same time, Mr Argento was suggesting that the club should effectively be wound up and the papers sold, even though this would not produce a large sum, and Mr Curtis was in agreement. It was perhaps only a matter of time before enough members were brought round to this way of thinking for the club to vote in favour. The result would be that Mr Bradstreet's hoped-for fortune would never materialise.

'Bradstreet decided to have one last attempt at locating the site of the treasure. He made a fair copy from memory of the salient points in the collected papers with the intention of pursuing his researches at the Scottish National Library in Edinburgh. And there, as it so chanced, he received the help and advice of Mr Stewart, a man who not only specialised in the history of the old families but had encountered similar enquiries before. There, Mr Bradstreet learned to his dismay that the story of the McClartondale treasure was no more than an historical romance. And worse still, there was a very strong indication that the papers the club had purchased were worthless forgeries.

'Mr Bradstreet returned to London and decided to share his discovery with the two members of the club he counted as his closest friends, Scordell and Geeson. Between them, they determined to make further enquiries to confirm their suspicions, before advising the other members of the situation. By doing so, they unwittingly alerted the attention of an extremely dangerous man.

'We may never know who Scordell decided to consult, the gentleman he met with on the day of his accident in Gresham Street. But we know that he met this man, presumably one who was not a member of the Explorers' Club, since he did not name him. Did he only hint at his concerns, or did he go so far as to entrust him with the club's secrets? That meeting led to his fatal fall. It might have been an accident, but it could also have been murder at the hands of the gentleman he met or another individual we know nothing of.

'Soon afterwards, Geeson received a message purporting to be from Bradstreet. I say purporting because we have not been able to examine it. The message suggested they meet at Alexandra Palace pleasure park. While there, Geeson witnessed the death by shooting of the unfortunate Mrs Thompson and realised that this might well have been an attempt on his life. He fled in a panic. He most probably dropped his yellow handkerchief, and it was picked up by the man who had tried to shoot him. A few days later, Scordell died in hospital without revealing any more information about his fall.

'Bradstreet, who was not aware that Geeson had gone away, sent a coded note of warning by his servant to Geeson at St Paul's. But the message was never delivered. He received no reply and went to St Paul's and was told that Geeson had left London. He may well have assumed that Geeson had received the note and had acted upon it and was therefore safe.

'And then, Stamford, you entered the story and alerted me to the mystery of the man with seven toes on his right foot. Our enquiries led us to Bradstreet, and he realised that Geeson never received his warning message. He hurried at once to St Paul's to warn his friend, and there he was killed by the same man who attempted to shoot Geeson, summoning him to his death with the yellow handkerchief. But who killed Bradstreet and how he came to be there at just the right moment, I cannot yet say.'

Suitably refreshed, we proceeded to Canon Alley where there were three shops to view, the first two of which did not look promising. Neither had a workshop on the premises, and when we enquired, both proprietors directed us to Berman's. Holmes naturally wanted to pay more attention to Berman's, where we knew there was a workshop and where the questioned document had originally been sold.

Mr Berman was an aged man, heavy and slow moving, like a sailing ship making its way through deep waters. He was a dark presence behind the counter, clad in a long black coat and wintry hat, his wide face almost occluded with a great bush of hair, yet somewhere within that formidable shape was a smiling mouth, little laughter creases about the eyes and a rumbling voice that might with a little encouragement turn into a booming chuckle. We saw at once that Vambrook's judgement was correct; Berman's hands were distorted with arthritis that he must have suffered from for many years, and he would have been unable to carry out any fine and detailed work.

He at once recognised that we were students and therefore with only modest amounts to spend, but unlike so many tradesmen, this did not deter him from displaying his wares to us, as if in years to come, better dressed and with laden purses we might remember him and return.

On discovering that we studied science and medicine, he was happy to conduct us to the shelves of suitable books. As we studied what volumes were available, a door opened at the back of the shop and a young man emerged. There was a brief consultation with the proprietor concerning some work and he disappeared back into his enclave. 'His fingertips and cuffs proclaim his trade,' said Holmes. 'He is the repairer of documents. He is barely above twenty and cannot therefore be the man who forged the questioned material.' As he spoke the door opened again, but this time it was rapidly closed without anyone emerging, as if the person inside had peered out and changed his or her mind on seeing customers in the shop. Mr Berman left us to examine the books while he returned to the counter, where he slowly and almost certainly painfully wrapped a volume in paper and tied it in string. He then very laboriously wrote some words on a label, which he fastened to the string. A boy was waiting in one corner of the shop, one of the many who carried out deliveries for tradesmen in the area. He was handed the book, with some coins and instructions as to where it was to be taken, and he scampered away.

We made sure to look about to see if there were documents on sale, and like at Barnett's there were some under glass, and a cabinet of drawers. Here we saw bible pages, many of which were in the Hebrew script. Some, with delicate illustrations, were attractive enough to be considered works of art on their own, and they certainly looked aged. Once again Holmes made a minute inspection, but without arriving at any conclusion.

He purchased a volume on anatomy, and we thanked Mr Berman and left. 'There is certainly room in either Berman's or Barnett's for a forger to ply his trade undetected,' he said. 'The two businesses might well deal with each other, depending on the interests of their customers. But we have no evidence of any criminal activity by the proprietors, and I would not wish to hint at it, lest we provoke suspicion against the wrong men.'

Before we departed Canon Alley, Holmes made another examination of Berman's window display. He then glanced at the doorway, above which the name of the establishment had been painted. This sign had been made many years ago, as it was very faded. I could just make out the letter S, after which there was a space, then 'BERMAN', the upper part of the capital b having been worn away by time. For some reason, Holmes thought this of interest, and approached for a closer look. Using his great height, he stretched upwards on tiptoes, and even took his magnifying glass from his pocket and extended it to the lettering. Then he stepped back with an expression of deep introspection.

'What is it, Holmes?' I asked.

'You can see the outward signs as well as I. The reason why I looked more closely.'

This was frustrating, as so many of Holmes' cryptic comments were. Was he testing me, to see if my powers of observation and deduction were improving? They could never reach his level, but I thought I had been making something of an effort in that direction. I wondered if he was simply demonstrating his superiority, which was one of his less attractive traits, and would have been infuriating in a less brilliant man. On the other hand, he might have been reluctant to say more at that stage, and I decided not to press him. He was testing the possibilities in his own mind, unwilling to say anything in advance of being certain to his own satisfaction. Holmes liked nothing better than being right, and nothing was more galling to him than being wrong.

'What will you do now?' I asked.

'I intend to return home and smoke a pipe,' he said. And that was all he would reveal.

CHAPTER TWENTY-NINE

When I think back to one of the most dreadful experiences of my life, I can recall quite sharply how well that day began. Yes, the nights were drawing in as one might expect for the time of year, and the clear skies had brought a chill to the darkness of late afternoon, but the sunlit hours had been uncommonly and unseasonably glorious. Newspapers were proclaiming how kind nature had been to the sporting events of the season, and the public were out promenading in droves, almost as if it had been summer. I felt disinclined, however, to attend the trotting races at Alexandra Park, and after my final lecture of the day, I hurried home in the deepening dusk, longing for my desk and books, glowing coals, toasted muffins, and hot soup.

While the area just north of Smithfield had something of a reputation for poverty, this was mainly due to the dilapidated and unsanitary conditions in some of the narrow courts and alleys leading from the main streets. I had never felt concerned during my walk home, negotiating the expanse of the old meat market and passing the numerous inns and busy workshops of metalsmiths and printers. The street where I lodged was alive with trade and manufacture, noisy and boisterous at times, but no more a threat to body and purse than many another thoroughfare.

It must have been recent events that led to my feeling unsettled that day. I had not been lured to any unexpected meetings by private notes and should not therefore have experienced the uncomfortable sensation that I was being watched and quite possibly followed. I was tempted to pause and look over my shoulder more than once, but this was in itself a hazardous business, and I decided I would be better off moving as quickly as I could to the safety of my rooms.

The door to the stairs which led to my apartment was in a small, sheltered entrance way, and as I approached it, key in hand, I saw a boy, one of the street urchins that ran about on broken boots all over London, standing nearby, leaning against the wall, almost casually. He appeared to be waiting for someone, and I was struck with the impression that he was waiting for me. When he saw me, he cocked his head and grinned. His cheeks were grey and streaked with dust, his nose a grimy button. I stared at him and made to pass him by, but he moved onto the pavement in front of my door and addressed me.

'Want a message taking, sir? Parcel carrying? All done as quick as you like.'

I was obliged to pause and was about to say that I wanted no business of that kind, and he should think of going elsewhere. But I had no opportunity to speak. At that moment, someone emerged from the darkness, stepping up behind me, and a long powerful arm clamped itself about my body, pinning both my arms to my sides, while a hand pressed a damp cloth to my face, so strongly that I felt my neck was about to break. He dragged me back off the street and into the seclusion of the entrance way.

The boy cackled with laughter and ran away.

The cloth was unmistakably impregnated with chloroform. I had smelt its pungent vapour in the operating rooms many a time, when it is carefully diluted with a large volume of air to make it safe. More importantly, I had recently read descriptions by the royal anaesthetist John Snow of criminal attacks and their outcomes. These had been quite amusing as a study but were a lot less amusing now. Snow had reported that the victims of such assaults, even ones unfamiliar with the properties of chloroform, will always do two things. They will hold their breath and struggle. Unless much weaker than their attacker, they will usually escape. It they cannot, they risk inhaling the concentrated vapour which would be instantly fatal.

A surgeon needs a clear head in difficult situations. He is trained to deal with emergencies, though usually these are emergencies that happen to someone else. I did my best to keep calm and purposeful. Naturally I held my breath, fearing that even a little inhalation might make me lightheaded. And then I made every effort to tear myself from my attacker. That was when any shreds of confidence I might have mustered left me. I struggled and strained but to no effect. To my growing horror I found that I might as well have been clutched in the iron grip of an armoured warrior, or the apelike arms of a creature more used to thrusting corpses up chimneys in the Rue Morgue. I tried kicking and flailing with my legs, but my inhuman attacker easily lifted me from the ground to make even that ploy ineffective. I began to sweat with blind helpless fear. Escape was impossible.

I could not hold my breath much longer. Sooner or later, my need to inhale would be the final irresistible act that would instantly stop my heart. I battled for calm, to know what to do, but all I could think of was to use the last of my strength, every ounce I possessed, to make one last determined attempt to break free. I let myself go limp very briefly to gather my energy and my resolve. There was one more try to make and then I was spent. And then, to my surprise, the cloth was removed from my face. I had the impression that the man was stuffing the horrid rag into his pocket. My eyes were stinging, but I was alive and conscious. It was a moment or two before I realised what had occurred. The sudden relaxation of my muscles must have made him think the liquid had taken effect. He thought I was asleep. One thing I knew about my attacker — he was no surgeon.

There was a shadow of a chance that I might be able to get away, but I decided, as a stiff breeze carried the last of the vapour from my skin and I ventured to fill my lungs with air again, to continue the imposture. I remained limp, and kept my eyes closed. I expected to be lowered to the ground, have my pockets rifled for coins and other valuables, and then left lying there while the thief departed. That was when I would be able to escape.

This, however, did not happen. The man, who was as strong an individual as I have ever encountered, easily turned me about, lifted me and flung me over his shoulder. One simian arm was now clasped about my legs; his other hand formed a steely manacle around one wrist. My other arm dangled free, but since I was not clasping a deadly weapon, I did not attach any hope of escape to this circumstance.

To my amazement, my captor now proceeded to walk with me in this undignified and helpless position. Since I knew the area even in the darkness, I was aware that we had turned a corner and were going north along Turnmill Street. Where he might be headed, I could not imagine. What did he want with me? All kinds of unpleasant and unsavoury thoughts crossed my mind, but I comforted myself with the idea that had he wanted to kill me he would have done so by now, and my best chance of escape was to continue the pretence and wait for my moment.

I was able at least to open my eyes and look about me. We were passing some of the many hostelries in that area, where the noises coming from within suggested that I was unlikely to be able to alert anyone who might be inclined to help me. One or two men, already well into their cups at such an early hour, were wandering about the street, but took no notice of me as I was borne along. The sight of someone carrying an apparently unconscious man over his shoulder was not, I realised, a novelty which might attract some attention. I wondered briefly what Holmes might do in such a situation, but then reflected that Holmes was far taller and stronger than I, not to mention an accomplished swordsman and boxer, and who knows what else, whereas I was merely a competent medium pace bowler.

We continued north, approaching Clerkenwell Road, but my captor showed no sign of stopping. I heard a train rumble on its way along the metropolitan railway below and wondered idly what its occupants might think of my plight had they known of it. And it was then, quite suddenly, that the full horror of my situation struck me. Holmes had said that the killer was adept at making a murder appear to be an accident. Only a few weeks ago an inebriated youth had fallen to his death on that same railway line, tumbling from the Ray Street Bridge not far from Turnmill Street. Even closer, however, was the Clerkenwell Bridge. Now I knew my intended fate.

There was a brief pause as my captor stopped, and I heard him gasp as if catching his breath. At this I almost thought of struggling again, but I was still held immobile in a grip of iron, and there was no-one about who might help me. He moved on. The only individual nearby was a man in the soiled and reeking clothes of an ironworker, walking with the satisfied amble of the moderately intoxicated, and clutching a bottle from which he was diligently refreshing himself. By now, my heart was thudding so hard with terror that I was amazed my captor could not hear it. My only advantage was that he still thought I was unconscious. However, if he did intend to throw me over the bridge onto the railway line, there was nothing I could do to stop him.

The drunken man was about to pass us, and as he saw me, he laughed and raised the bottle as if to toast my dedication to drink. I had just one chance and I took it. I reached out, snatched the bottle from his hand, and dropped it on the pavement. The shattering glass made a highly satisfying sound.

This noise and the loud roar of fury from the bottle's owner were enough to alert my captor, who whirled about to face him. This saved me from the worst of the assault, as the drunken man made an angry attack on us both with flailing fists. With a grunt of annoyance, my captor dropped me to the ground. I did my best to maintain my pretence as I thudded onto the pavement, but fortunately he was sufficiently distracted not to notice any stifled exclamations. I heard the unmistakable sounds of a fight between him and the inconvenient obstacle. I didn't look, I didn't hesitate. I started to my feet and ran as fast as I could. My legs were weak and trembling, and could scarcely support me, but I was young and terrified for my life. I did not run home, but north, turning onto the busier thoroughfare of Clerkenwell Road, where I hoped to find help. I must have looked like madness personified. Luckily, I saw a hansom cab and quickly attracted the attention of the driver, who must have seen nothing more than a man in a tearing hurry in need of a ride.

The cab stopped, and I gratefully flung myself inside, gasping out the one address where I instinctively knew I would be safe. I looked out of the window as we drew away, but the lamps revealed nothing of my attacker or the drunken man who had inadvertently been my saviour. I collapsed in a corner, my chest heaving, my head thudding, my legs folding beneath me like those of a marionette. Fortunately, I was a little recovered when I reached my destination, but how I must have appeared as I stumbled out into the quiet of Montague Street, I could not imagine.

CHAPTER THIRTY

It was only when I was safely in Holmes' rooms, clutching a tumbler of warm brandy and water while seated before a fire which he had heaped generously with fresh coals, that I realised how much every part of my body ached. Holmes allowed me some time to gather what was left of my nerves so I could tell him what had happened. I must admit that when I described the violent attack, my helplessness in the powerful hands of my assailant, and what I had feared would be my inescapable fate, I gave way to a torrent of emotion. I know that men may weep manly tears without any sense or accusation of shame, but I am sure I blubbered like a child.

My injuries, such as they were, did not prove to be great. I was bruised, of course, and over the next few days marks would appear and darken where I had been grasped and held in that crushing grip and from being dropped to the ground. There were cuts and scratches I could not recall having received, my neck and shoulders ached, and my eyes were sore. Most visible, however, was the reddened skin around my mouth from the contact with liquid chloroform, which I hoped would not lead to blistering.

I asked Holmes to tell me the worst since I dared not look in a mirror. 'I can't appear at college looking like this!' I wailed. 'What will everyone say? I can't even go to the police — what can I tell them?'

'All you can remember of this person was that he was a very strong man and entertained an unreasonable expectation of the action of chloroform,' said Holmes, drily. 'That is a large proportion of the male population of London.'

'I am so sorry!' I exclaimed miserably.

'But you are alive to tell the tale, and by your own efforts,' said Holmes. 'Do not make light of that.'

'I have told you nothing useful at all,' I said.

'On the contrary, I can make something of it. The man who attacked you is either someone we know or was hired by him. He has been alerted to our enquiries, and I believe that his attempt on you was a warning to me. He must have thought he had a better chance of success in dispatching you, and believed that having done so, I would be afraid to continue my investigation. He clearly does not know me well if he thinks I can be frightened into inaction. He also employs a messenger boy, perhaps more than one. These ragged little creatures know the streets of London and can go swiftly about without being noticed or remembered. They are as common as flies, and as dirty, but far more useful, with sharp ears and sharper eyes, and will carry out any task for payment. I wish I had an army of them. Our man probably knows you are a student at Barts and had you followed to discover the location of your lodgings, and a suitable place to make his move. There, he, or his minion, lay in wait. You say the boy addressed you? That was to ensure you stopped and were distracted so his master could come up behind you for the attack. He is a strong man, as you said, but he was not confident he could match you for speed if you were able to avoid him.'

In such a moment I know Dr John Watson would have seized his service revolver and set out to boldly tackle his enemy. I was not made of his sterling material. 'I can't go home,' I cried. 'He knows where I live. He might try again. He might try anything!'

'I expect he has used similar means to discover where I live, too,' said Holmes, casually.

'Where will you go?'

'Nowhere. I will stay here. I will be alert to the dangers, of course, but that is all I shall do. But I agree that you should not go to lectures for a while. Your nerves are quite broken down, and you should rest and wait for your bruises and the marks on your skin to heal. By then, perhaps the culprit will be under arrest, and you need not fear him.'

'Do you know who he is?'

'I have my suspicions,' he said, eyeing a mark on my wrist bone which had all but broken the skin, 'but I hesitate to say any more at present, since the case is not complete. In the meantime, I suggest you stay with George Luckhurst. He lives not far from here, and I can arrange to take you there and deliver you safely. I will also provide you with books and lecture notes so you will be occupied and not fall behind with your studies.'

That sounded like the best way of proceeding. Holmes decided to accompany me there as soon as I had finished my brandy and water. Despite the lateness of the hour, I had no stomach for any food. I confess that I was a little concerned at arriving at Luckhurst's lodgings unannounced, as his devotion to the customs of Ancient Greece occasionally extended to adopting forms of their clothing when at leisure in his home. Although he and Holmes had been at college together, I doubted that Luckhurst had ever been found in his rooms wearing a chiton, which even for a student of classics might have excited some comment.

'What shall we tell him?' I asked.

'He will see at once that something is wrong, and I suggest you say that you were the victim of a failed robbery which has left you bruised and shaken. If you go on to say that you prefer not to discuss it in detail, I am sure he will understand.'

And so, indeed, it turned out. Luckhurst, who I was relieved to find was clad as decently as any Englishman might expect and require, was pleased to see us, dismayed at my dishevelled and miserable appearance and delighted to have me stay. There was more than enough food and drink on hand for the three of us to make a nice supper, especially as I still had almost no appetite and had to be persuaded to take a little much-needed sustenance.

'You may stay as long as you like,' said Luckhurst. 'But I ought to mention that I will be away for a week from tomorrow morning. There is a museum in Brighton which has recently acquired some very interesting sculptures, and I am being sent there to study them. It is quite an honour. In the meantime, you must treat my home as yours. I will provide you with a key so you may come and go as you please. The landlady, Mrs Godstone, is very kind. If you ask her, she will bring you anything you want.'

'If you should need anything for your studies, Mrs Godstone should have no hesitation in alerting me,' said Holmes. He turned to Luckhurst. 'And Stamford will, I think, prefer to have no visitors apart from myself. Anyone else who wishes to visit him should first be approved by me. Neither will he want to be troubled by any of those little ragged creatures who carry messages. If one such should ask for him, Mrs Godstone should say he is not here.'

'Of course,' said Luckhurst, who if he was surprised at these requests did not reveal it. 'She will not allow them in the house in any case; they are all dirt and who knows what else. She says they all look the same to her, like a swarm of rats.'

My mind, still afloat with the warm brandy that was dulling my pain, was dreamy with images. Did the boys who ran messages really all look the same, I wondered? They all had dirty faces, hands, and fingernails, black with filth, but they were clad in different species of discarded clothes of all sizes. Some were without shoes, others bound their feet in greasy rags, the luckier ones had boots salvaged from rubbish heaps, or stolen. I thought that had those same little messengers been washed and properly clad, they would rather have resembled that line of schoolboys I had seen on the day when we visited headmaster Bradstreet, boys who reminded me of my own schooldays. And then, another memory sprang to mind of something I had seen that day. Seen but not observed, and never thought to mention to Holmes. It had lain forgotten until that moment.

'Holmes,' I said. 'On the day when I followed Bradstreet to St Paul's, there was a boy, a messenger boy. He followed me as I walked, and then he ran past me, and ran past Bradstreet too. After that I saw no more of him, and I suppose I didn't think about him again. But I have the feeling — I think he was the same boy I saw outside my home last night. Just before — just before what happened.'

Holmes was struck silent by this information, and for the next few minutes he was deep in thought. Both Luckhurst and I knew better than to interrupt him. 'Of course,' he said at last. 'I see it all now. The place, the time, it all fits.'

'I thought at first he was following me or Bradstreet, but of course he wasn't,' I said.

'Describe him to me,' said Holmes.

I did my best and he nodded.

Luckhurst was staring at us. 'Stamford — that boy must know who it was who tried to rob you,' he said.

'Yes,' said Holmes. 'But leave it with me. I will make some enquiries and see where it leads us.'

When Holmes decided to go home, I was able to have a brief word with him while Luckhurst removed the dishes from the table. 'I am rather glad that Luckhurst will be away. He will be in no danger in Brighton. Do you think you have the answer now?'

'I do. As you know, I have been wondering since Bradstreet's death how his killer chanced to be waiting for him at St Paul's when that day's visit was unplanned. I believe now that the boy you saw was hired to watch Bradstreet. He was running to tell his employer that his quarry was on his way to the cathedral. Either he was already at St Paul's, or he was simply nearby. He is the same man who killed Scordell and tried to murder Geeson. And now I am sure I know who he is.'

CHAPTER THIRTY-ONE

Holmes was as good as his word. During the next few days, everything I needed to pursue my studies was delivered to me. He had informed the college that I was indisposed following an accident and did not want visitors. Holmes also paid me the occasional visit, bringing copies of lecture notes he had borrowed from other students. He advised me only that his enquiries were proceeding to a conclusion but provided no further details. I was naturally anxious, but he reassured me that he was taking every precaution to ensure that no-one knew where I was staying while preserving his own safety. He refused to reveal the identity of the man he suspected.

Sometimes Holmes tried to distract me from my own woes and fears with conversation on other subjects. He talked about his growing enjoyment of music, and how, when his purse permitted, he would haunt the great concert halls to experience the finest exponents of the violin the world had produced. Of his own proficiency with that instrument, he said only that his practice was continuing, and he hoped in time to be able to produce something melodious and pleasurable to the ear. He had been making a study of violins, learning how to distinguish the best of them from those of inferior manufacture, and was hoping that his own instrument, which he had purchased for fifty-five shillings from a shop in Tottenham Court Road, was rather more valuable than it had appeared. I asked if he might consider having it evaluated by an expert, but I am not sure he ever did. Some years later, he boasted to Watson that it was a Stradivarius worth 500 guineas. Whether that was true or just his fancy, I never discovered.

Mrs Godstone, a motherly lady, supplied me with all the nourishment I required and more. It should have been a contented existence, but I knew it could not and should not last.

One afternoon Holmes paid a call, and I could see he was expecting something or someone, but what or whom he would not say. We talked about medical matters, until a gentle knock at the door told us that the housekeeper was outside. She brought a gilt-edged card, which Holmes perused. 'Ah, yes,' he said, 'Mr Argento. I had expected him to come sooner or later.'

'Will he be admitted?' I asked nervously.

'Yes,' said Holmes. 'I believe he may have all the answers I require. Show him up, please, Mrs Godstone.'

'How did he know where I was?' I asked.

'I permitted him to discover you,' said Holmes. 'It was essential that matters be brought to a head.'

I was still reeling from this information when Argento appeared, puffing at the exertion of climbing two flights of stairs. When I heard that little convulsive gasp of breath, I almost jumped up and ran from the room. I had heard it once before, but on that occasion, I had been draped over the shoulder of a man who intended to kill me. Holmes saw my panic and gave me a reassuring glance. I made a concerted effort to calm myself. This time, I was not alone and helpless.

Argento declined any refreshment other than being able to rest in an easy chair, which he did, stretching out one leg in front of him with a wince of effort. Being familiar with Luckhurst's unusual decorative tastes, I had forgotten how outré the room might appear to a stranger. I saw Argento stare about him in curiosity, taking in the Grecian styled statuettes, etchings of classical subjects and the ornate frieze over the mantlepiece. I expected him to comment but he did not do so.

'Mr Holmes, Mr Stamford,' he began, 'I believe the time has come for us to engage in a frank and open discussion.'

'I agree,' said Holmes, calmly. 'We have a great deal to learn from one another.'

'And I hope we may thereby come to an understanding of where we might proceed after today.'

'That is my intention,' said Holmes.

'Might I suggest that you begin by telling me what you know?'

Holmes nodded. 'I will start by describing what I have deduced of your history. It begins with the opening of the shop in Canon Alley by your grandfather, a Mr Silberman. The original sign has faded over the years, which has led many customers to assume that the family name is Berman, but a close inspection reveals otherwise. Your grandfather was a skilled bookbinder and repairer, and I can imagine that from an early age you sat by his side and learned his secrets, while your father, who was not so adept, operated the business. It was a skill that came naturally to you, and which you continued to develop. When your grandfather died, he left behind his workshop, his tools and materials, and in you, an understanding of his methods. But your father must have had other ambitions for you. He would have recognised your intelligence and believed that you could advance both yourself and the family through education. It was not an easy thing to achieve financially, but I imagine he applied all the family resources to that end.'

I saw Argento nod. 'He did. I was the only son,' he said.

'The death of your mother at the hands of the banker Arnold Haxby was a turning point in your life. You became strongly aware of the prejudices which could place obstacles in your path and control your destiny. You must have realised that you would have a better chance of achieving your ambitions with a different name, a different identity. Silberman, silber being the German for silver, became the Italian, Argento, also meaning silver.

'Over the years, your hatred of Arnold Haxby never diminished. You determined to learn all you could about him and bring down this powerful man. I had wondered how you chanced to be at the same university as his son, but it was not entirely chance, was it? One of the things you must have discovered was the college where he had studied. When you applied for a place at university it was to this same college, most likely in the hopes of learning something you could use against him. I don't know if you knew he had sent his son to the same college, but that was how you met Alban Haxby, who was a younger version of his father.'

'Yes,' said Argento. 'You are quite correct in all you have said so far. I strove to know that scoundrel better. One should always know one's enemies; how else might one learn their weaknesses? My masquerade as being of Italian descent has served me well. I made valuable connections, men who would have despised me if they had known the truth. I cultivated living a life of lies until it became second nature to me. I invented a wealthy father, who lives abroad and is a collector of Roman antiquities. I am, as you see —' he gestured to his ample figure — 'no athlete, not even then. I could not compete on the field, but when I knew Haxby was a rower I thought I could join that fraternity, since I am unusually strong about the arms and shoulders, and in those days, my legs served me better than they do now.'

'What I am not sure of,' Holmes went on, 'is how you first encountered the story of the McClartondale treasure.'

'I found the volume amongst a collection of books my father purchased from a Scottish gentleman,' said Argento. 'It was of small value, but I saw its possibilities.'

'And the copies of Webster's dictionary?'

'Acquired by the shop from a sale.'

'You forged the papers, did you not, the ones that you fed piece by piece to the Explorers' Club?'

He laughed. 'I did. I was young and still developing my skills. It was a form of exercise, I suppose. It amused me.'

'But then it became something more.'

'Yes, and very quickly. I recognised the naked greed of young Haxby and decided to draw him in and show him up for the ignorant fool he is. I dropped a paper onto the floor of a bookshop and made it appear that it had been lodged between the pages of an old book. Haxby picked it up, and my work was done. I was intending to reveal my trickery in time, but what I did not anticipate was the interest of the others. Some were simply in need of money, existing on a meagre allowance until they could support themselves, others like Haxby sought riches, but had no desire to work for them, and the rest just craved adventure.' He smiled modestly. 'I am not a leader of men. It was easy for me to fade into the background and allow Haxby to direct things. They consulted me occasionally, that was all. I even urged caution. No-one saw me pulling the strings. The Explorers' Club was formed, and all the members agreed on how it was to be run, a division of profits according to the size of investment. When I was home during the long vacation, I produced more papers and fed them gradually to small dealers and auctioneers. The club purchased them. I made a little money from it, but none of any great consequence. No, my main pleasure was knowing that I was playing for fools men who would not have given me the time of day, men who thought that violently pushing aside a poor defenceless Jewish woman was their privilege, their right. Each purchase stimulated more interest, more greed. After we left college, we continued meeting at Haxby's club.

'Secrecy was, of course, essential. No-one else was to be admitted. We were enjoined never to speak to outsiders of the Explorers' Club, even to our closest friends and family. It was not hard to introduce the idea that there might be others who were pursuing the same quest but without our resources at their disposal. A careless word might be fatal to our fortunes. Our little coded messages afforded me considerable amusement.' He uttered a laugh of sheer contempt. 'So much seriousness and application to a worthless enterprise.'

'The real reason for the secrecy,' said Holmes, 'was that you dared not risk an expert examining the papers.'

'Indeed. My youthful efforts would not have deceived an experienced man.'

'But you continued to perfect your skills over the years,' said Holmes.

Argento's vanity got the better of him and he beamed complacently. 'Indeed. I saw a place in the market for documents of which I could take advantage if I applied myself. I became highly adept at forging ancient Hebrew manuscripts, which were accepted as genuine by the most demanding collectors and sold for high prices. Under the circumstances, I rather wanted my lesser apprentice works to disappear in case they aroused suspicions and led to me.'

'Were your forgeries sold through your father's shop?'

'Yes, he sells on commission. I told him I had been going to sale rooms and examining collections, purchasing documents I thought I could repair and sell at a profit, and had made some promising acquisitions. You were in his shop one day when I was at work. I saw you but I did not enter. It might not have been obvious, but my father's eyesight is not as keen as it once was, although his mind is as sharp as ever. I could not risk trying to sell such important papers through another dealer in case I aroused suspicions. My father, on the other hand, based on my assurances, accepted my documents as valuable discoveries. He and all my family, my dear sisters, and their husbands, are quite blameless. My father has lived many years suffering the loss of my poor mother, but the idea of revenge never entered his head. He is a gentle soul.

'To my friends I represented myself as an agent for my wealthy Italian father, searching the galleries and dealers for the artefacts he desired. Friends did occasionally see me entering my father's premises in Canon Alley, and I was obliged to explain that it was necessary to use some unsavoury sources to find what I sought. Haxby said he hoped I was clever enough to cheat a Jew. I said I would do what I could. It is a common boast amongst men such as he. I often use it myself; it is a useful barometer by which I measure those about me.'

'It was you who stole the papers from the Mansion House vaults,' said Holmes.

'It was. Haxby — even a fool has some uses — told me what Musgrave had said about you and your little adventures in detection at college. I know I had a worthy adversary, and of course I dared not risk you seeing the papers. I had had a copy of the key to the strongbox made long ago during one of the times it was in my possession. I was also able to get a locker key copy made. I took a wax impression from Haxby's key, one evening when he was drunk, which was not a rare occurrence. I removed the papers from the box and burnt them.'

'I have had suspicions for some time that the forgeries should be laid at your door,' said Holmes. 'I have not mentioned these suspicions to anyone else. I can see that to do so might bring disgrace and disaster to your family.'

'It would, and I am grateful for your silence. I live very simply, Mr Holmes. I am not one for the ostentatious luxuries of life. My lodgings are simple but pleasant; I have a club where I like to dine. All my letters and messages are directed there. But most of the time I am at work, doing what I enjoy most. You may think I am a villain, but the money I have made from my forgeries was hard earned.'

'What I cannot condone, on the other hand,' said Holmes, 'are the murders you committed to conceal your other crimes.'

'And now we come to it,' said Argento. 'Do you happen to have a gun about you, Mr Holmes?' Before Holmes could reply, our visitor took a small revolver from his pocket. 'If you do, I beg you, take it out and point it at me. It would make my task so much easier.'

CHAPTER THIRTY-TWO

No man should have to stare down the barrel of a gun which is in the hand of a cold-blooded murderer. I looked at Holmes, who appeared quite unconcerned by this development. Perhaps, I thought, clinging to a hope born of rapidly mounting panic, he didn't mean to kill us; this was just to ensure he was able to escape.

'I do not have a gun,' said Holmes. 'And I might remind you that this is not an opportunity for you to commit a crime that appears to be an accident, and with which you cannot be connected. I am well aware of your usual way of proceeding. Your presence here is known. If you harm us, it is extremely probable that you will be apprehended, and the subsequent investigation will reveal your true identity.'

'And yet,' said Argento, 'how else might I be certain that you will remain silent? You have been a danger to me for some time, and I wish to ensure that you are no longer. But I agree, Mr Holmes, I cannot risk exposure, not only for myself but for my family. Who would believe them innocent? The suspicion alone would be fatal to my father.'

'And this was why you stooped to murder? To protect not only yourself from a long prison term, but also your family?'

'It was.'

'You do not work for anyone else?'

'I do not need to.'

Holmes looked disappointed at this reply, but then his expression hardened. 'You are a very dangerous man, Argento. Even if this is not the most convenient time for you to murder us with any hope of escaping detection, and you depart today without causing us harm, we will probably spend the rest of our lives trying to anticipate when and where the blow will fall. But before you make your plans to destroy us, I would appreciate it if you could enlighten us on the facts of your murderous schemes. I would at least like to be reassured that my deductions were correct.'

Argento smiled and nodded. 'I suppose I owe you that satisfaction, at least. But first, I have to make sure of something.' He eased himself out of the armchair, still with the gun pointed at us, keeping his distance in case Holmes made a sudden lunge. I looked at Holmes, but he did not appear to be about to make a move.

Argento went to the door, opened it briefly, and glanced outside. 'I would not put it past you to have half the police force listening on the stairs, but I can see that we are not being spied upon.' He closed the door and as he returned to his seat, he cast his eyes briefly over some pages of notes I had been working on which were still lying on a little writing desk. He smiled but made no comment before he sat down. 'Let me see, where to begin?'

'Mr James Scordell,' said Holmes.

'Ah yes, poor fellow. I thought well of him, but he was too much of a danger. A few weeks ago, Scordell asked to consult me in private. He wanted me to confirm my agreement that the Explorers' Club enterprise should be wound up. I told him of course I would. Then he said that the papers should be valued by an expert and sold. I said I could arrange that. Naturally, I was more than able to provide suitable sale certificates which would be accepted as genuine and repay the Club members what they had spent. Then —' Argento uttered a sigh of regret — 'he incautiously revealed Bradstreet's visit to Edinburgh and what he had found there. He told me that both he and Geeson were concerned that the papers were not genuine, and an expert examination would expose them as worthless forgeries. He wanted to know precisely where they had been purchased and see the documentary evidence. Given Mr Scordell's profession and his association with an art gallery, I could see that anything of that nature I might offer him would be most carefully examined, and there was a very real danger they would be found not to be evidence of actual purchases. He even revealed to me that Bradstreet had made a private copy of the papers, which he now had in his possession. Then he mentioned the document which had recently been displayed in the gallery and which had been proven a forgery, thus engaging his concern that there might be others. It was, as you might have deduced, one of my earlier works carried out before I had perfected certain processes. Scordell had even begun to suspect that it might be a work by the same man who had created the McClartondale papers or an associate of his, that there might be a little workshop hidden away somewhere manufacturing this material. He meant to launch an enquiry. That was his fatal mistake. I feared that everything I had so carefully constructed was about to collapse. I promised to provide him with the papers he wanted if he could let me see the notes Bradstreet had made, and then we would meet again to discuss what we had found.'

'You met him in Gresham Street?'

'Nearby. I suggested that to allay any suspicions of our purpose, we should walk and talk like two men on a convivial stroll. I had already planned what I would do. I asked to examine Bradstreet's notes, saying that I wished to do so out of curiosity to see how accurate they were. He suspected nothing until we walked past the burnt-out warehouse, and I set the notebook alight and threw it into the still smouldering ruins. He stepped forward to rescue it and I pushed him hard. It worked even better than I anticipated. I thought he might stumble over the edge, but instead the whole floor was so weakened it collapsed under him. I almost fell in myself and jumped back just in time. I was a little alarmed when I learned later that he was still alive, but he was too badly injured to reveal what had happened. I went to see him in hospital to check. By then, he was unable to recognise anyone. All the same, I thought it advisable to hurry him along a little.' He raised one large hand towards us, palm facing. 'It was the kindest thing.'

I shuddered.

'He did reveal your name,' said Holmes, 'only I did not realise it at the time. He said he had met "Argento", but the nurse who attended him thought he had said "a gentleman". I cannot blame her, but I should have been more alert. And then, you turned your attention to Geeson.'

'Yes, he was a considerable danger, given his work with old documents. I had read in the newspapers about the shooting galleries at Alexandra Park and thought what a fine chance that would be. I bought the gun and sent him a message he thought had come from Bradstreet, about watching the bicycling. Dangerous things, bicycles. Best avoided. I told him where to stand to attract my attention, and what with all the crowds it was easy to find cover where I could lie in wait. But then that silly woman and her children passed by, and he must have turned his head. I missed him and hit her instead. The excitement did enable me to get away, and I found Geeson's yellow handkerchief where he had dropped it in his fright and picked it up. One never knows when such a thing will be useful, and so it proved.'

'Then you were told that Geeson had gone away.'

'Yes, that was a disappointment, but I determined to wait my chance. In the meantime, I engaged a boy to watch Bradstreet and tell me where he went. I know he went to St Paul's hoping to see Geeson soon after he left, and that gave me an idea. I guessed he would return after a time, and he did. So, yes, Mr Stamford, that was I you saw on the whispering gallery waving Geeson's handkerchief. I seized Bradstreet by the ankles with the result you saw.'

'And when you realised that we were on your trail, you attempted to murder Mr Stamford,' said Holmes. 'Your ring left a notably large bruise on his wrist.'

Argento frowned. 'Yes, that was my second failure. I rather expected the chloroform to be effective for longer. Perhaps I didn't use enough.'

I opened my mouth to correct him, but Holmes gave me a sharp look and I was silent.

'And now, here we are,' said Argento, 'in this so charming location, and looking about me, I think I can see my way forward. I admit that I was unprepared when I came here for the unusual character of the decor. What a remarkable little sanctuary this is. How delicious. How very private!'

'You won't get away,' said Holmes.

'Oh, but I will. The tragedy of your deaths will appear to be the result of a quarrel. Such things are not unknown between gentlemen of your —' he hesitated, his eyes resting for a moment on an extremely tasteful etching of a Greek vase depicting a pair of Olympic wrestlers '— aesthetic persuasion. Rivalries and jealousies in such society do occur, even between the very closest of friends. This will appear to be such an incident. I am sorry, but I simply cannot trust either of you to remain silent. Therefore, I am obliged to shoot you both. It will appear that one of you shot the other, and the survivor, overcome with grief and remorse and having penned a note of explanation, has then turned the weapon on himself.'

'You can't force either of us to write such a thing!' I exclaimed.

'Really, Mr Stamford, I forge medieval documents.' He glanced at my papers. 'I think a suicide note would not present me with any difficulty. Once you are both deceased, I will rush to alert the housekeeper and send her to fetch a policeman. That will give me ample time to arrange everything in the room to tell the sad story. And, of course, I will have been an unwilling witness.'

My energy seemed to drain into my boots. I could only hope that Holmes would know how to save us both. He was about to say something, but at that moment there was a knock at the door. I recognised the careful tapping of Mrs Godstone.

Argento grunted in frustration. 'Tell her to go away,' he said.

'I will not,' said Holmes, calmly.

'Very well, then we will wait for her to leave.'

'I think she will be well aware that there is no violent quarrel in progress,' said Holmes. 'Your plan may not proceed as you intended.'

'Mr Holmes? Mr Stamford?' said Mrs Godstone. 'There is an Inspector Hardiman of the City of London Police who has arrived and wishes to speak to Mr Argento. I told him he had called and was here still. Shall I show him up? He is very insistent.'

'Please do,' said Holmes.

It was obvious to Argento that his plans to murder us had gone awry. He took a cloth bag from his pocket and put the gun inside it. Then he thrust the gun into a drawer of the writing desk. 'And now,' he said, 'where is the evidence that this gun was ever mine? I have taken careful steps to ensure that it can never be traced to me.' He resumed his seat with a smile of triumph.

Mrs Godstone admitted Inspector Hardiman, who, like Argento, was initially disarmed by the elegance of the apartment. 'This is not your home, Mr Stamford,' he said.

'No, I am looking after it for a friend who is a scholar of classical art.'

He nodded. 'Ah, I understand. Well, Mr Argento, I am glad to have found you. We have been making some enquiries regarding a fatal incident which took place in St Paul's Cathedral. A friend of yours, a Mr Bradstreet, fell to his death in circumstances which are not yet fully understood.'

'Oh dear!' said Argento with a nice appearance of genteel dismay. 'That was a dreadful business, but I really cannot imagine how I can assist you.'

'That remains to be seen,' said Hardiman. 'What I would like is for you to accompany me to the police station, where we will take a statement. I have a cab waiting outside.'

I thought of the gun in the drawer. It was pointless to reveal that it was Argento's, and he had been about to kill us with it. He might even try to suggest that it belonged to George Luckhurst. I said nothing.

'Why, of course I will accompany you, Inspector,' said Argento. 'I will do anything in my power to help you.'

Hardiman and Argento descended the stairs under the eye of Mrs Godstone, who was lurking nearby. Holmes and I followed. I think Holmes was concerned in case Argento made a sudden attempt at escape, but he did not. Instead, he and Hardiman climbed into a cab, most of which was occupied by a large constable, and drove away. I think I almost collapsed with relief.

'Come,' said Holmes, 'let us get you inside. I am sure Mrs Godstone will provide hot tea. A drop of Luckhurst's Greek brandy would not come amiss, either. But there is one thing I must do first.'

And then I saw, leaning against the railings, the little snub-nosed boy whom I had seen passing me on the day Bradstreet died, and who had confronted me so very recently. To my amazement, Holmes tossed him a coin. The boy put it in his pocket and ran away.

'But — that's Argento's messenger!' I exclaimed.

'Who better to keep an eye on Argento for me without him suspecting? Those ragamuffins know nothing of loyalty; they will work for whoever pays them. They turn their coats for a sixpence.'

'Then you knew that Hardiman would come?'

'I did, although not the precise moment of his arrival. He ran it a little close.'

We returned to the apartment for much needed refreshment. Holmes removed the gun from the drawer and after a brief examination, extracted the bullets and put both the weapon and its ammunition in his pocket. 'Fully loaded,' he said. 'He took no chances. What a desperate villain!'

'I cannot help thinking that it was the death of his mother that took all the heart from him,' I said. 'How young he must have been when he lost all capacity to feel anything for another person.'

'Such men are rare. They may seem to be as others, which makes them doubly dangerous.'

I wondered if I ought to refer in some way to Argento's error of judgement about Holmes and myself stemming from the Greek decor but as I essayed a comment, I received a glance from Holmes which ensured my silence on the subject forever.

I fully expected to learn that Argento had been arrested and charged with murder, but on the following day we were summoned for an interview with Inspector Hardiman.

The inspector took careful note of all Holmes was able to tell him, but concluded, as had Holmes, that there was no actual evidence against Argento, and nothing with which he could be charged. Ruben Argento, after hours of detailed questioning at the police station, had been allowed to depart. Nevertheless, Hardiman made it very apparent that he intended to keep a close watch on him in future.

CHAPTER THIRTY-THREE

I never did discover the fate of the drunken man whose intervention had saved me from certain death. No body was found, so I assumed that after his tussle with Argento he had been allowed to lurch on his way and had very little recall of the incident. Like Geeson and me, he had had a fortunate escape.

As far as we knew, Argento was living very quietly in an effort not to attract the attention of the police. Holmes suspected that he might be planning to flee abroad. I rather hoped he would. His villainy was now out in the open, and he had nothing to gain by harming either Holmes or myself, but I still feared a reprisal.

I returned to college more or less healed and deflected a number of suggestions from my fellow students that I had suffered my injuries through excessive drinking. This was so out of character that no-one really believed it. I told them I had fallen from an omnibus. No-one believed that either.

A week later the decomposing body of a plump, well-dressed gentleman was seen floating serenely down the River Thames, where it passed through the central arch of Blackfriars Bridge. A police constable was alerted and summoned assistance. The body proceeded in a westerly direction, and finally came to rest near Temple Pier, where it was recovered. On examination, it was found that the skull was fractured so badly that a piece of bone had entered the brain. Extensive damage to the face had rendered the deceased unrecognisable. He was identified only by his clothing, which bore laundry marks, and a distinctive item of jewellery, a gold ring formed like a Roman coin, and was declared to be Ruben Argento, a dealer in antiquities. Attempts were made to contact his family in Italy to give them the sad news, but they could not be located.

The inquest, presided over by Mr Payne, determined that the man had not died by drowning. It was thought that he had jumped into the river from one of the recesses of London Bridge, and fallen headfirst onto one of the abutments, causing instantaneous death. When Argento's lodgings were searched, a note was found stating that he was about to go on a long journey for the sake of his health. The verdict was suicide due to temporary insanity.

The sparse contents and the simplicity of the deceased's rooms were much remarked upon, especially by those who knew him. There were a few bank books which showed a small sum invested, and a purse of coins, but nothing else of value. There was also an unpaid bill, the total sum being due to Morris Silberman of Canon Alley for commission on sales. It so chanced that the total effects found were just sufficient to meet this bill, which was duly done. Argento, it was said, liked people to think he was rich, but this was far from the truth.

Argento's most startling legacy, however, was a set of documents and reports which showed that he had for some years been assiduously enquiring into the history and professional activities of the Haxby family, employing both a detective and an accountant. It was speculated that it was this activity which had swallowed up any fortune he might have had. The results were turned over to the police. The outcome shocked society and filled the sensational newspapers for several weeks. Arnold and Alban Haxby, father and son, were both arrested and charged with embezzlement from the bank. Lengthy prison sentences and the destruction of their good name and personal wealth were to follow.

Mr Geeson, having learned of Argento's death and the circumstances that preceded it, returned to his duties at St Paul's Cathedral library. A few months later, he heard that his father had died after a short illness at the age of sixty-two. This information had come not from his stepmother, but a neighbour in Lincolnshire who wrote to him at St Paul's. By the time the letter arrived, the body had already been buried. It was not long before questions were raised about the death, since the new wife not only stood to inherit the whole of the estate but was also due to receive a substantial sum in insurance. The body of Geeson senior was exhumed and found to contain a fatal amount of arsenic. Despite vehement protests that her husband had taken the arsenic himself, either in error or in a deranged fit of self-destruction, the wife was arrested and tried for murder. The trial was an unpleasant and squalid affair. The evidence consisted of the prisoner's possession of arsenic, an insurance policy taken out only a week before the husband's death on which it was suspected that his signature had been forged, and rumours that she was conducting an affair with another man. Despite interrupting the proceedings with loud assertions of innocence, well-larded with expletives, she was convicted of murder. Local opinion was unanimous that this was the right result. Since a murderer cannot profit by his or her crime, the widow was overlooked, and Geeson received his inheritance.

A large crowd assembled outside the prison on the day of the hanging. According to the newspapers, the atmosphere was more appropriate to a festival. It was said that had the execution been carried out in public, as was traditional in the old days, the crowds would have been larger still. Geeson was now master of the estate, but his heart was not in Lincolnshire, and he sold the property for a handsome sum. He lost no time in proposing marriage to the lady who had earned his affections and she accepted him.

Miss Ellison, as Holmes had predicted, remained anxious not to waste any more time in bringing a man to the altar. She had continued to entertain hopes of Holmes, but finding he remained impervious to her allure she was obliged to cast her net wider. Mr Bradstreet senior, perhaps looking for comfort and companionship in his declining years, was bold enough to offer his hand. She might well have accepted, but young Bullstrode, he of the college rowing crew, had arrived home from Darjeeling, brown as a nut, and with enough money to open a tea import business. They were engaged within three months and married soon afterwards.

Mrs Scordell was safely delivered of a healthy son, who was christened James, with Mr Vambrook standing proudly as the child's godfather.

As far as we were able to discover, Mr Curtis never reached the heights to which he aspired. He was able to climb a little further up the ladder of government service, but on reaching that rung where he just exceeded his natural abilities, he remained in place thereafter in a state of permanent disgruntlement.

Mr Tibbott's father reached the end of his patience and declined to meet any more his son's gambling debts. Tibbott, after failed attempts to win back his losses, turned to other means of making his fortune. A few years later he was arrested for passing false cheques, and imprisoned.

One evening, Holmes, Luckhurst and I had enjoyed a pleasant dinner, followed by a convivial glass of Greek brandy, when Holmes, in an uncommonly good mood, began to speak of the fate of Ruben Argento. Luckhurst had fallen into a doze, and

Holmes felt able to speak freely. 'Did it not seem a strange coincidence to you that Argento had managed to make over all his portable property to his father? The bill was of course one of his forgeries, but I am sure his father understood its meaning.'

'I suppose he could not write a will without arousing suspicion of the family relationship,' I said. 'But my greatest surprise was his making away with himself. I never thought he was the type. He always seemed to plan everything with such care.'

'Including his disappearance,' said Holmes. 'The broken skull of the corpse was only assumed to have resulted from a fall. It might have been from another cause entirely.'

It took me a few moments to understand Holmes' meaning. 'You think the body was not Argento's?'

'All the evidence points to it. If a desperate man wants to disappear so he is thought to be deceased, he might try to find an unsuspecting victim to take his place. Anyone grateful for the gift of a good suit of clothes and a gold ring. Argento only needed to find someone of about the right build. Knowing that the body would probably be found and examined, he had to persuade the man to cleanse himself in the public baths before donning his new attire. Then the man was lured, perhaps with the promise of drink, to the right location and dispatched.'

'That means he has murdered again,' I said, sadly.

'A less troublesome scheme might have been to appear to vanish in some dangerous location such that even if a body was not found, his death would be easily assumed. Either way, no-one will come looking for him.'

'If you are right, then I wonder where he is and what he is doing now,' I mused.

'He has valuable skills, so I assume he will be up to some kind of mischief,' said Holmes. 'The world has not heard the last of Ruben Argento.'

HISTORICAL NOTES

Sir John Abernethy (1764–1831) was a surgeon at St Bartholomew's Hospital. His well-attended lectures led to the founding of the medical school. Sir John is said to have suggested adding a little sugar and some caraway seeds to an otherwise plain biscuit, thus creating a popular snack intended to aid digestion, which still bears his name. There are many recipes available, and the author could not resist baking a batch! https://larderlove.com/abernethy-biscuits/

The Abernethian Society, founded in 1795, was a students' club for the reading and discussion of medical papers. It held regular meetings in a reading room usually referred to as the 'Abernethian Room', and this name survives to this day as that of the new common room of the Students' Union.

The coded message Holmes mentioned to Stamford was described in "The Adventure of the *Gloria Scott*".

The unusual deaths described in chapter 2 are all to be found in inquests reported in the newspapers of the 1870s, apart from the death of Scordell, which is fictional.

William John Payne (1822–1884) was coroner for the City of London in 1876.

The Trevors of Donnithorpe appear in "The Adventure of the *Gloria Scott*"., which Holmes solved during his college vacation. The Musgraves of Hurlstone feature in *The Musgrave Ritual*, an adventure Holmes described to Watson which took place during his early years in London, and which Stamford clearly did not share with him.

William Palmer, the poisoner, was hanged in 1856. Holmes mentions him in *The Adventure of the Speckled Band.*

The McClartondale family is fictional.

The Explorers' Club mentioned in the book is a fictional association of college students and is not connected with or intended to represent any actual society. The Mansion House Club is also fictional.

John Snow (1813–1858) is best remembered nowadays for identifying the cause of cholera epidemics as contaminated water, in defiance of the then current theory that it was spread by bad air. He was a pioneer of safety in the use of anaesthetics, establishing the necessity of carefully controlling the concentration of the vapour in air. His great work on the subject is *On Chloroform and Other Anaesthetics* (1858), in which he advised that the vapour should ideally be diluted at 4 per cent by volume in air. At 8–10 per cent by volume, inhalation can result in stopping the action of the heart and sudden death. His letters to *The Times* in 1850 on the criminal use of chloroform included several examples of the outcome of attacks such as the one experienced by Stamford, exposing the popular fallacy (which still exists, as so many films and television dramas demonstrate) that simply placing a chloroform pad on the face of a victim produces almost instant unconsciousness. Further information on the use and misuse of chloroform can be found in this author's book *Chloroform: The Quest for Oblivion* (The History Press, 2005).

In 1876, chloroform deaths during or following surgery, some of which occurred days after the actual administration, were often stated to be due to a fatty liver.

Watson mentioned Holmes' violin in the first novel, *A Study in Scarlet*, published in 1887. It was not until later that Holmes boasted to Watson of his clever purchase of the instrument, which he believed to be a Stradivarius, in "The Adventure of the Cardboard Box", first published in 1893. Watson described the seller as 'a Jew broker', but whether this was an accurate report of Holmes' actual words or Watson's paraphrase, we cannot know. The author, who is Jewish, realises that there are some aspects of the Holmes canon which make uncomfortable reading nowadays.

A NOTE TO THE READER

The timeline of the events in the life of Sherlock Holmes in the canonical fifty-six stories and four novels has occupied, fascinated and sometimes frustrated Holmesian scholars for many years. The most commonly accepted year of Holmes' birth is 1854. He did not meet Dr Watson and occupy 221b Baker Street before 1881.

Almost nothing is known about his early life and very little about his education. I think it is possible that, like Conan Doyle, he spent a year at school on the continent, where he acquired his knowledge of modern languages. He is known to have spent two years at a collegiate university, which means either Oxford or Cambridge, although which one, and what courses he took have never been revealed, but he did not take a degree. The year in which he settled permanently in London is unspecified. His first recorded case is that of "The Adventure of the *Gloria Scott*", as recounted to Dr Watson, which took place during the university vacation. Holmes had been developing his powers of observation and deduction and was known amongst fellow students for his singular method of analysing problems. At the time this was nothing more to him than an intellectual exercise. During his work on the *Gloria Scott* mystery, however, it was suggested to him that he would make a brilliant detective and that idea took hold and gave him a direction in life.

Holmes realised that he lacked the broad and varied fields of knowledge which would serve as a foundation for his mental skills. The next few years were dedicated to acquiring that knowledge, and in doing so, he created the man who burst upon the literary scene and met Dr Watson in the first Holmes novel, *A Study in Scarlet*.

In my work, I have suggested that Holmes was at university during the years 1873–75, solving the *Gloria Scott* mystery after his second year. Realising that his particular requirements could not be provided by a university course, he did not return, choosing instead to undertake his own studies. He had boxed and fenced at university and while there is no evidence that he devoted dedicated practice to either later on, it is clear that these were skills he retained. His lodgings in London's Montague Street placed him close to the British Museum where he must have spent many hours studying in the library, and he enrolled at St Bartholomew's Medical College for practical courses in chemistry and anatomy.

And that is where my series begins.

Reviews are so important to authors, and if you enjoyed the novel I would be grateful if you could spare a few minutes to post a review on **Amazon** and **Goodreads**. I love hearing from readers, and you can connect with me online, **on Facebook**, **Twitter**, and **Instagram**.

You can also stay up to date with all my news via **my website** and by signing up to **my newsletter**.

Linda Stratmann

2021

lindastratmann.com